*The Lovers
Set Down
Their
Spoons*

The

Iowa

Short

Fiction

Award

In honor of

James O. Freedman

University of

Iowa Press

Iowa City

Heather A. Slomski

The Lovers Set Down Their Spoons

University of Iowa Press, Iowa City 52242
Copyright © 2014 by Heather A. Slomski
www.uiowapress.org

Printed in the United States of America

The University of Iowa Press is a member of Green Press
Initiative and is committed to preserving natural resources.

Printed on acid-free paper
ISBN: 978-1-60938-282-7 (pbk)
ISBN: 978-1-60938-299-5 (ebk)
LCCN: 2014935650

Contents

ACKNOWLEDGMENTS

I would like to thank Stuart Dybek and Jaimy Gordon, the best teachers a young writer could hope for. I am so fortunate to have studied with them and to have them as mentors today. I would also like to thank my WMU peers—talented writers and good friends—who critiqued three of these stories in workshop, especially Maggie Andersen, who has been reading my work ever since.

I would like to thank Paul Griner, Jeffrey Skinner, and Brian Leung for awarding me the Axton Fellowship in Fiction at the University of Louisville, for giving me two years to write in a city I love and miss, and for their continued friendship and support.

My deepest gratitude to the contest readers from the Iowa Writers' Workshop for sending my manuscript up the ladder; to Wells Tower for choosing it as the 2014 Iowa Short Fiction Award winner; to copyeditor Will Tyler for his patience and his careful reading; and to Jim McCoy, Allison T. Means, Charlotte Wright, and Karen Copp at the University of Iowa Press for all of their hard work in bringing this book into being.

Thank you to my parents and siblings for their encouragement, and to my Aunt Kate for her keen editorial suggestions.

Finally, I am forever indebted to my husband, fiction writer Vincent Reusch, for reading my revisions of these stories again and again, for his insightful comments, for inspiring me with his own work, but most of all for Oscar, our little ginger-haired boy.

Grateful acknowledgment is also made to the following literary journals for publishing these stories from the collection: "The Lovers Set Down Their Spoons" first appeared in *The New Guard*; "The Chair" in *Columbia: A Journal of Literature and Art*; "A Seat at the Table," "Women," and "Octaves" in *Tri-Quarterly* #121; "The Allure of All This" in *TriQuarterly* #126; "Correction" in *Knee-Jerk*; "Iris and the Inevitable Sorrow or The Knock at the Door" in *The Normal School*; "Silhouette" in *Velocity*; "A Fulfilling Life" in *Isthmus Review*; "Blue Door: A Collection of Passings" in *Poet Lore*; "Adrift" in *Ascent*; and "Rescue" in *Sawmill*.

The Lovers
Set Down
Their
Spoons

The Lovers
Set Down
Their Spoons

──────────────
███████

We are sitting at a table in a restaurant. The four of us. You. Me. The woman with whom you had an affair. Her boyfriend. I sit across from her, you across from her boyfriend. There is wine, red and white. There are four water glasses, four linen napkins, four spoons, eight forks, four knives. There are tables on all sides of us.

Behind the bar a large mirror reflects the brilliance of a chandelier.

The woman with whom you had an affair: (looking at you) How did you find this place?

You: I read a review in the paper. The owners live upstairs—they keep a six-hundred-square-foot herb garden in planters.

The woman with whom you had an affair: Six *hundred* square feet?

You: Incredible, right?

The woman with whom you had an affair: I'll say.

Her boyfriend: (butters his bread).

The waiter had brought olive oil for our bread, but he, her boyfriend, asked for butter. I liked that about him.

I wonder what he is thinking—the boyfriend—staring now at the couple one table over: she in a below-the-knee red dress; he in corduroys and a striped dress shirt. I imagine the boyfriend is wondering if they are lovers. Perhaps if they are both lovers first to someone else and lovers only second to each other.

She isn't beautiful—the woman with whom you had an affair. Coarse and a bit squat, she's not at all the woman I'd imagined.

The woman with whom you had an affair: (looking at her menu) Everything looks so good. Good restaurants always make me wish I cooked more. But by the time I even think of dinner it's too late to make anything, so Simon and I usually order in Greek or Thai. (She watches you for your reaction.)

Simon: You hate Thai. You're allergic to peanuts and coconut milk.

The woman with whom you had an affair: (pretends not to hear Simon; she sips her wine and is noticeably relieved when the waiter arrives).

Waiter: (white shirt, black apron, tall, and long-limbed) Something more to drink? Perhaps an appetizer?

You: (taking charge) Yes, we'll have the fried sage leaves and . . . ahh . . . (poring over the menu) an order of the squash flan.

Waiter: Very good. (He leaves the table in long, thin steps.)

The woman with whom you had an affair: Great choices. Simon and I love flan. Don't we, Simon?

Simon: (sips his wine).

You: I order flan whenever it's on the menu.

I notice a slight trembling of the chandelier, as if someone is walking upstairs in the spice cabinet where the owners live, bending between the rows of herbs—plucking.

The waiter arrives with the appetizers and sets them in the middle of the table. You, the orchestrator of this event, lift a sage leaf onto each of our plates with your fork and knife. With your spoon, you slop piles of squash flan next to our sage. The three of us pick up our silverware, but you are unsure of what to do with yours. They've been designated serving utensils. Can you eat from them?

I poke the sage leaf with my fork and bite a third of the leaf. It looks and tastes like a fried anchovy. I grab my water and try to swallow the fish like a vitamin, but I (*cough cough*) choke a little and spit the fish into my water glass.

You: (ignoring me) Oh, this is great. Have you tried the sage? (You are looking at her—at the woman with whom you had an affair.) Have you tried the fried sage leaf?

Through the windows the sun is setting. It is nearing eight o'clock and the last rays are reaching through the glass. They are sliding down the panes like a coat of sheer gold paint, and the restaurant seems to float in this buoyancy of light. I hate New York. I am beginning to feel a sick longing for my before-life—when I lived in Boston and I didn't know you.

Me: Simon. What do you do?

Simon: Taxes (breath). I do taxes.

Me: What do you do for fun?

You and the woman with whom you had an affair look at me simultaneously, as if I have just said something wrong, awkward, inappropriate.

Simon: For fun?

Me: Yeah, for fun.

Simon: I play cards—I'm in a bridge club. I golf, go to the movies. Just bought a new bike.

The woman with whom you had an affair: We were in Seattle a couple weeks ago and saw—what is the name of that film (she turns to Simon)—that Spanish one—oh you (she looks from you to me) really have to see it. What was it called, Simon?

Simon: I don't know. I'm glad I forgot. (He looks at me.) If you're into movies where people are so obsessed with books they masturbate in library bathrooms, then maybe you'd like it. (He sets his fork against his small, blue plate.)

You: (looking at her—at the woman with whom you had an affair) Are you talking about the one with *lighting* or *making light* in the title?

Make light, I think. Make light. What words, I wonder, did you use with this woman? Fuck? Have sex? Intercourse? Make love? Make light?

The woman with whom you had an affair: Yes! *Making light of it* or *lighting it*—wait, maybe it was Danish.

Simon: Swedish. (He turns to the table next to us. The woman's fork catches the last of the sun as she lifts it to her lover's lips—if he's even her lover. He almost chokes, and they are laughing.)

The waiter takes our order, and when he's finished he closes the sun into his black book. Another waiter hurries around the restaurant, holding a cigarette lighter above the tea candle on each table. I watch Simon yawn, and the gold cap on his back tooth twinkles in the candlelight. Something about the gold in his tooth (I turn to look at you) makes me think of the absurdity—the absurdity of us.

You: (to her, of course) Are you reading anything? Anything good?

The woman with whom you had an affair: In the last week or so I've accumulated so many new books that Simon and I barely have room to walk.

Simon: (turning briefly from the lovers) I don't have problems walking.

I stand up to find the restroom, but your foot is in the way, so I kick it.

You: (leaning forward) What the—

Me: (I look at Simon, then at the woman with whom you had an affair.) Excuse me. (Turning to you) I'm sorry, did I catch your foot?

You: (squinting) That's all right. It was an accident.

Me: Of course it was. (My voice sounds like cranberries.)

Small squares of light drip from the ceiling and illuminate my path to the WC. A few paces ahead, a waiter is slowly approaching. He is balancing two bowls of soup on his right forearm and holding one in his left hand. He looks so young—his red hair sticking up by his ears because someone cut it too short. His belt is the smallest rubber band, holding up his pants like tying a balloon.

Me: (slowly and evenly toned) Careful, I'm right here—right in front of you.

The young waiter: (lifting an eyebrow) I see you.

Me: Do you want me to—

The young waiter: No. I have to do this on my own.

I step aside, and he passes by. I watch him walk along his tightrope to deliver the soup. He makes it.

When I am back from the WC, our meals arrive, and the waiter sets them before us, admiring our choices. He leaves, and I look down at my plate. My pasta is green, too pretty to eat. I push my plate forward and reach for the wine bottle. I begin to pour and the waiter rushes over—mortified that my fingers touched the bottle. I wave him away.

Me: (to you) What?

You: (whispering sternly to me) He would have done that, you know. In places like this you're supposed to let *them* pour your wine.

Me: (to you) Places like *this*? Like *this*? (I'm not sure why the repetition.)

I watch you cut your meat and sprinkle your salt. Sometimes you're a vegetarian, and sometimes you're not.

Simon: (taking a bite of his *tre funghi penne*) This is terrible. I hate mushrooms. (He pushes his plate away.)

The woman with whom you had an affair: I don't know why you ordered it, then. (She lifts an asparagus spear to her teeth.)

I had a neighbor, years ago, who cultivated asparagus. Locked out one scorching afternoon, I knocked on his door and asked to use his phone. My boyfriend at the time had the only other key, and when I reached him he told me to stay at the neighbor's or climb through a window. When I repeated this to my neighbor, he said not many people know this, but asparagus is actually a member of the lily family. Come, I'll show you. We walked through his house and into the garden. That night when my boyfriend brought over the key, I broke up with him. Did you know, I said, that under ideal conditions an asparagus spear can grow ten inches in twenty-four hours? I'd forgotten about my neighbor until tonight.

Simon: I always think *this* time I'll like mushrooms. (He leans back in his chair.)

You: (to the table) This lamb is amazing. (*Chew chew chew.*) Mary had a little lamb, little lamb, little lamb? Mary had a little lamb whose tush is on my fork.

The woman with whom you had an affair: (smiling and blushing) That's so mean!

I look to Simon to return my expression, but he's engaged with the lovers.

The lovers: (Her long arms reach across the table for his face, and he drops his chin into her palms).

I've forgotten what it's like to feel a range of emotions in a single day.

Waiter: (bowing) Is something wrong?

Me: Wrong?

Waiter: With your pasta dishes?

I shake my head no, and Simon does the same.

Waiter: (annoyed) Very well, then. I'll wrap these up.

You and the woman with whom you had an affair finish eating, and the waiter takes our coffee order.

Simon: (sugar, no cream).

Me: (cream, no sugar).

The woman with whom you had an affair: (black).

You: (after debating between Earl Grey and coffee, you order coffee—black).

The waiter follows his outstretched arms into the kitchen and a few moments later appears with a tray of coffees. One by one he lowers a cup and saucer from above each of our heads like birthday cakes we aren't expecting. Then he leaves and returns with the dessert tray.

Waiter: (leaning forward) This is the raspberry-ginger sorbet. This is the prune tart. This pretty one is the Chinese Lantern. This—with the ladyfingers—is the Accordion. This is the Brooklyn Brownie. And this is a petite madeleine.

The woman with whom you had an affair: (sucking in her stomach and patting it) Just coffee for me.

Simon: (to the waiter) Do you have any lemon tarts?

Waiter: No, sir. Only what I have here on this tray.

Simon: You're sure there aren't any lemon tarts stuffed in the back of the freezer?

Waiter: No, sir. We only serve homemade desserts that are baked fresh daily.

Simon: What are they having? (He points his thumb at the lovers.)

Waiter: (leaning to the side in order to see past Simon) Looks like they got the last pear flambée. We're discontinuing that dessert after tonight.

I look over to the lovers. Two spoons. Two mouths. Ten fingers—five his, five hers—entwining themselves in each other. A bit over the top, I agree. She reaches for his wrist and turns it toward herself. Clearly they are late for something, because the lovers set down their spoons. They weave through the tables—their raincoats billowing out behind them like the kites you and I flew on that terrible day that began our love. Your kite kept wrapping around mine, and at first I thought it was sweet, but eventually mine nose-dived into the sand. I knelt down beside it as the waves crept closer, wanting to take the kite—a small sailboat—out to sea. Your kite was still up in the air, and you were balancing yourself beneath it. *Look! Look!* you yelled. *Watch how it twirls!*

I turn around in my chair to face the door, but it's too late. The lovers are gone.

Me: (looking at Simon) Where did they go?

You: Who? Where did who go?

Simon: To a movie.

Me: I doubt it.

You: (to the woman with whom you had an affair) Who are they talking about?

The woman with whom you had an affair: Simon, who are you talking about?

The waiter leans over the table and places the bill in the middle. You and the woman with whom you had an affair begin grabbing at each other's fingers.

You: (swiping the black book from her grip) You bought last time, remember? Those burgers that were bigger than our plates? (With these words you pause and look at me.)

Me: (whispering) I'm embarrassed.

You: (your hand on my shoulder) I'm sorry. I shouldn't have brought it up. We can still—

Me: I'm embarrassed that you would be interested in someone like her. I'm nothing like her.

You: (looking around for the waiter, because you won—your credit card made it inside the black book, and you want him to take it) Of course you're not—there's no one like you. (You raise your hand awkwardly, as if you're hailing a cab for the first time, and you're not sure you're doing it right.)

Me: But tell me. I want to know what you saw in her. Oh, who am I fooling—what you see in her.

Simon: (pointing at you with his pinky) Hey—I'm embarrassed that she would be interested in someone like him.

You: (to Simon and me) Who the hell do you two think you are?

I laugh out loud.

You: Listen. The affair came about because there were problems, and now there aren't. We're handling this in the best way possible. (You look from me to Simon.) Both of you agreed to this.

I am laughing harder now, and I snort once.

You: (to me) What? What is funny?

Me: (blowing my nose in my napkin and looking at you) You are funny. I am laughing at you.

The lover: (appearing behind the woman with whom you had an affair) Have you seen a pair of glasses?

The four of us look up at him.

You: What the hell is going on here?

The lover: (to you) Look, buddy, I'm just looking for my reading glasses. I thought I left them on my table, but they're not there.

Me: (to the lover) Where is your—

The lover: She's out there (he points to the door) waiting for me. Just forgot my glasses—that's all. Anyway, I'm sorry. I didn't mean to interrupt.

Me: Oh. (To you) I was just about to say that I'm not going to be with you anymore.

You: (pointing at the woman with whom you had an affair) Because of her?

The woman with whom you had an affair: (opens her mouth slightly, as if she might say something, but she closes it and slowly reaches for her coffee cup).

You: (to me) Come on, you don't mean it. You're just upset.

Me: But I'm not upset. I've been upset for three years, and I'm not anymore.

You: What are you talking about you've been upset for three years? I only saw her (again, pointing at the woman with whom you had an affair) for six months.

Simon: (to the woman with whom you had an affair) Six? (He looks from her, to you, then back to her.) You mean you two didn't get your story straight before our big night?

The woman with whom you had an affair: (reaches into her purse and pretends she is looking for something very important).

Simon: (to me) You want to split a cab?

Me: No. Thanks.

Simon stands up.

Me: (to Simon) But I'll walk out with you.

You: (to Simon and me) I knew it—I knew it all along. I knew you two were seeing each other.

Simon starts for the door, the lover follows him, and I follow the lover.

Me: (to the lover as we step into the night) But I don't see your—

The lover: She's holding a cab somewhere . . . (he scans the curb). There she is—see?

The lover's lover is pushing against the grill of a taxi to keep it from moving forward. The driver is yelling and swearing out his rolled-down window.

The lover's lover: (calling from the street) Are you ready, my love?

The lover: (to Simon and me) Well, looks like we're off.

The lovers disappear into the yellow of the taxi, and the taxi (huffing and puffing and chugging along) disappears into the side mirrors of other taxis.

Me: (to Simon when we can no longer see the lovers) It was a pleasure meeting you.

Simon: And you.

I take a step backwards and a *crunch!* erupts from beneath my foot.

Simon: What was that?

Me: (quickly) Nothing.

Simon: You stepped on something. I heard it.

Me: I'm afraid to look. I know what it is.

Simon: (Bending down to the pavement, he picks up the lover's glasses.) You snapped off the right arm.

Me: (taking the glasses and holding them up to the streetlamp) The lenses aren't cracked. (I look more closely.) There's not even a scratch. (I fold the left arm and carefully place the glasses inside my coat pocket.) I should get these to him. He probably can't read without them. Where do you think they went?

Simon: I don't know where lovers go.

Me: (stepping backwards toward the restaurant) I'll check inside. He might have left his information with the host. Maybe I can catch him before they've gone too far.

Simon: (handing me the broken arm) You should take this.

Me: Thanks. Well. I guess this is goodnight.

Simon: Goodnight.

After a brief handshake, I watch Simon walk down the street, becoming smaller and smaller before getting into a cab. I reach into my pocket and pull out the glasses. I set them on my nose and fit the left arm behind my ear. Hazy shapes begin fusing and breaking apart, like organisms on a microscope slide. My eyes focus, and the images sharpen. Then: clarity. The world stops. The streetlamps turn red. And the moon, as you would expect, is enormous.

The Chair

We bought a chair at the flea market from an old man who was selling all the things he did not want. It was a square chair—red and white checkered—and although the old man had had the chair for forty years, it looked brand new. My husband sat down in the chair, patting the arms comfortably with his hands. I paid the old man fifty dollars, and since we had only a small Volvo and he a large truck, he said he'd deliver the chair to our house on his way home from the market. I asked him was it out of his way to do so, and was he sure that he didn't mind? He said that he only does things that are out of his way— that this was his new approach to the world. We appreciate it, I told him, and wrote down our address. If we weren't home, he said he'd leave the chair on our front porch. My husband shook hands with the old man. Then we moved deeper into the mixing colors of the flea market: what looked like smashed stained-glass windows glued into lamps, a bed frame made from bamboo, a wooden train set with a red "Whistle Works" painted on the caboose, a strawberry plant, an Italian stovetop coffee maker. I'd be happy with a cup of coffee, my husband said, and we headed back through the market. We saw that the old man's things were no longer there, so we figured that he had packed up and gone now that the sun was setting. We drove home through the city, and on the way I noticed a woman leaning out her apartment window, watering the onions in her window box. There was nothing unusual about this because we lived in a city where to have a window box was to have a garden. I remember one summer watching a man grow eggplants out his bathroom window. I think it may have been the only window in his whole apartment, because why else should he choose the bathroom to grow vegetables? When we got home we saw the old man's truck parked in front of our house, and we figured that he was on the porch—perhaps just setting down the chair. But as we stepped up onto the porch we saw that he was in fact sitting in the chair, weeping. Hands over his eyes, he jolted at the sound of my shoes, and I immediately apologized for startling him. Don't apologize, he said, what do you have to be sorry for? And I felt like a mime at that moment because my hands were moving, but I had no words. My husband awkwardly moved toward the old man sitting in his—no, our—red and white checkered chair. If you don't want to sell us the chair, he said, it's all right (even though I knew that deep down my husband really wanted the chair). But the old man said, it's your chair—how am I to leave with your chair? I may have been a lot of things in my life, but I was never once a crook. At this point there was a long pause. No one had anything to say, and the old man kept weeping. You could come for visits, I asserted. You could come to our house to sit in the chair. Thursday evenings, we could say. But the old man said, why should I come to your house to sit in your chair? Well, I half-whispered, why did you want to sell the chair if you are so fond of it? I sold the chair, the old man said, because I don't need it anymore. Why should a man keep what he does not need? Again there was a pause. Then why are you crying? my husband asked. And the old man answered, what else should a man do when he has just sold his chair?

The Allure
of All This

Anderson stood behind the counter in the men's section of the department store. He had arrived, as always, with a Styrofoam cup of tea that he hid on the shelf beneath the register. *No beverages across the red line.* Julian, his manager, had been instructed to paint a red line on the threshold of the break room. Since the nine o'clock hour Anderson had waited on one lady and one gentleman. A pair of striped socks for the lady's husband and a double-breasted suit for the gentleman. Anderson spent the day sorting, folding, hanging clothes, and with afternoon he grew tired in the glow of dress shirts surrounding him.

It was seven forty-five when Anderson turned the key to his third-floor apartment. He walked through the small living room and into the kitchen, where he set two brown bags on the counter. Ermalinda? he called. At the end of her name he heard the bathtub faucet screech on for a moment, then off. Ermalinda? he called again just before his knuckles rapped the bathroom door. Still no answer from his wife, so Anderson cracked the door and asked once more, Ermalinda? before he opened it and entered.

She was in the bathtub, covered in suds. One leg lifted and bent, her foot flat against the tiled wall above the faucet and a pink razor in her hand. She didn't look up. I've brought dinner, he said. Burgers, and steamed carrots instead of fries. Ermalinda ran the razor up her shin, over her knee, and up her long, soapy thigh. She did this on every line of her leg, and when she switched legs the suds parted, and Anderson could see her nude body like a calendar page floating in the bathwater. Ermalinda was long and thin, and the bathtub seemed to end too soon for her. Anderson was tall himself, but perhaps because he preferred showers and rarely bathed, his wife seemed extra tall—almost too tall—to be bathing the way she was in their bathtub. I'll be a few minutes, she said, still not looking up, though Anderson stood watching her, his long wife, in the bathtub. I said I'll be a few minutes, Anderson, she repeated. Right, he said, and closed the door behind him.

In the kitchen Anderson took the burgers from the boxes and set them on plates. Ermalinda walked into the kitchen in her white bathrobe, and Anderson dumped carrots next to the burgers. Then carried the plates to the table. The cabbage, she said, and Anderson pronged a layer of cooked cabbage from the pot on the stove and brought it to his wife in a bowl. I'll be working a lot this week, he said as he sat down. You probably won't see much of me. Ermalinda *mm-hmmmed* as she bit into her burger.

The next morning at the store Julian was especially chipper. We're getting in a new line of fall coats, he said to Anderson. Plaid raincoats and zip-up straight jackets in cornflower blue, powder blue, slate blue, and navy. And there'll be lined rain hats, he said, in every pattern you can imagine! Anderson looked at Julian. Can you picture it? Julian asked. This place will be transformed!

At eleven forty-five, the tailor arrived with this week's alterations, and he and Julian had their usual arguments about cut and price, shades of black, and whose mother came from a smaller town in Italy. Anderson grabbed his jacket from a hanger in the break room and rode the escalator down to the ground floor. As he descended he saw the transition that Julian was pushing on him this morning. It was July, and the half-dressed female mannequins were shedding their summer apparel in order to dress for fall. Their plastic breasts pointed ahead, waiting to be concealed by light sweaters and knit scarves. Anderson, they said, looking up at him. Come closer to us. We want to talk to you.

When he reached ground level, Anderson passed the mannequins on both sides as he walked toward the revolving glass door. He stopped, for a moment, at the brunette who stood to his left in a pair of white lace panties. If he touched her he thought she might move. Then she could sit across from him while he ate half a sandwich and slurped some noodle soup. If they went somewhere busy, no one would even notice, like that little place on Charles Street where you push your tray along the tracks and they have those high stools. He'd have to cover her with his jacket, but he wouldn't be able to—he'd have sweat stains on his shirt from walking. Anderson stepped past the mannequin and into the white light of the revolving door that pushed him onto the street.

He pulled a pear from his pocket and ate it as he walked toward Newbury Street, though he wasn't paying attention and instead found himself on a bench, looking across the Charles River to Cambridge. Sailboats in front of buildings, seagulls in front of sailboats—Anderson threw the pear core in a beautiful arc: a home run at Fenway, a swan-diving woman, the sun rising over the harbor and setting through the windows of the department store.

Circling through the revolving doors, Anderson entered Lingerie. He walked past the mannequins stuck in their gestures, and just before the makeup counters, he stepped onto the escalator and rode slowly up, feeling light-headed. Anderson, the brunette called to him. Don't leave. I am lonely, Anderson. I want to talk to you.

Anderson turned around to see her. So delicate and beautiful, she was getting smaller with each step that was sucked into the second floor. He looked at her—then at the shortening distance between himself and the top of the escalator—then back at her. He was caught. I'm sorry, he said without speaking. I can't.

Do we have any larges in these 401 Raindrops, Julian asked Anderson, who nearly walked right past him, not seeing him engrossed in a rack of men's dress shirts. Jesus—said Anderson. No. I sold the last one Monday. He continued walking to the sales counter, where he began folding the items that someone had decided against. He was stretching out the arms of a lavender shirt when he caught himself in the mirror alongside a male mannequin. What is it? Julian asked, a handful of ties hanging from his fist like eels. Have you ripped a seam? No, said Anderson, it's nothing, and he walked away from the counter with a pile of clothes to return to the shelves.

Mr. Sentry? Mr. Sentry! Julian called as he stepped through the door to the fitting rooms. This is nice, he said, holding a haystack green tie beneath Mr. Sentry's throat. Look into the mirror, Julian told him. Do you see the hazel appear in your brown eyes?

As Anderson rode the escalator to the ground floor he saw the exit light by the revolving door shining on the brunette, who was wrapped loosely in a short, black see-through robe. Anderson stepped off the escalator and walked toward the door. Hello, Anderson, she said. Come to me. He put his hands in his pockets and walked toward her. Don't worry so much, Anderson. You're only lost. Anderson looked through her lingerie. What's your name, he asked. Mia, she said. Mia, he repeated, and his phone began ringing in his coat pocket. It's Ermalinda, he said. My wife. Your wife, said Mia. Goodbye, Anderson. Anderson looked up at her—now still and mute. Wait, he said. He lifted his hand toward her face, almost touching her cheek. I'm sorry, he said as he stopped himself. Then he stepped into the golden light that circled him onto the sidewalk.

Anderson set his tea beneath the register and moved the bamboo shoots to the corner of the counter. Julian had brought them last week: three green sticks stuck in gravel and covered with water in a low rectangular pot. They're soothing, he'd said. Our customers should feel relaxed when they come here. You should, too, Anderson, though I know it's sometimes difficult.

Anderson—thank God you're here early! Julian rushed up to him. We're completely out of boxes. Can you check with Charlene? I've got to finish the orders, and I just don't have time. Sure, said Anderson, sipping his tea. Don't spill that, Julian winked.

As Anderson rode the escalator down, he straightened his tie and wiped his hands on his pant legs. He took a left into Women's, passing a mannequin with a pumpkin-colored shawl draped over her shoulders and a leather handbag dangling from her wrist. At the sales counter he asked Charlene for boxes. Here, she said, handing him a tall stack. We should be getting another shipment in soon. Thanks, said Anderson. Then he asked the price of the shawl. Seventy-eight—isn't it gorgeous? said Charlene. Yes, said Anderson, and he walked past the escalator into Lingerie.

The stack of boxes rubbing against his chin, he saw Mia. As he approached her he looked through her tiny purple dress to her triangle of panties. Out of boxes? Mia asked. Temporarily, Anderson said. You can check with Marcee, Mia said. Thanks, said Anderson, but this should be enough for now. I like that, he said, what you're wearing. Mia looked down at her body. I'm barely wearing anything, she said. You like what I'm not wearing. I just mean you look nice, he said, a bead of sweat sliding down his forehead. There's a shawl over there that I think would be great on you, he said. The one Cindy's wearing? Mia asked. It's stunning, she said. So classy. Yeah, said Anderson. Classy. Well I couldn't wear it, she said. Not here. Of course not here, Anderson said, but maybe outside of work. It's expensive, Mia said. I can't spend that kind of money. Can you have lunch with me later? Anderson asked. No, Mia said. You seemed too alone to be married. I wouldn't have called you over to me if I'd known you were married. Well you shouldn't be so careless, Anderson said. You really shouldn't. He turned around for the escalator and felt a little unbalanced with all those boxes. He felt like a baker balancing a wedding cake. Don't drop it don't drop it don't drop it don't drop it.

At the end of the day when Anderson took the stairs that exited through Accessories, Julian called down the stairwell: Anderson! Have a nice day off tomorrow!

Saturday morning, Ermalinda still asleep, Anderson opened his eyes and looked directly into the mirror that faced the bed. He saw Ermalinda's uncovered leg and sat up, gently touching it with his fingers. She felt chilled, and Anderson covered her with the quilt. He swung his feet out over the side of the bed, stepped into his slippers, and shuffled to the kitchen, where he peeled an orange at the breakfast table. Through the windows there was sun and a light breeze, and three stories below he saw a man happily carrying a duffel bag of clothes toward the laundromat. Orange peel uncoiling from his hands, Anderson looked through the lace curtains. The man nodded to the delivery guy walking toward him with a clipboard, and the two men lingered for a moment—a brief morning conversation.

Anderson dressed in the bathroom: khakis, a semi-casual dress shirt, and a light corduroy sports coat, and he left the apartment before nine, after which Ermalinda could be expected to wake. He walked down the street, stopping for a moment, to peer through the window of the laundromat at the man sitting on an orange-cushioned metal chair next to the circular hum of the dryers. He was reading something and drinking a Coke. He saw Anderson at the window, and Anderson gave him an awkward wave, then continued walking toward Park Street where he boarded the T and rode to Copley.

One leg forward, Mia stood with her hands on her hips. It's your day off, she said to Anderson. What are you doing here? Mia, he said, my marriage is a formality. I mean, it is now. We married young, and for a while it was youth, but for a long time it's been a formality. In bed we are two yellow beans under her reading lamp—nothing more. He reached for her hand. You shouldn't, she said. Her hair was pulled back from her face, and she wore a green bra and panties. You're beautiful, he said. Your wife, said Mia, what is she like? She's long, like you. Why do you ask? She reads a lot. Too much. Her mother's a real—well, it doesn't matter, he said. And Mia replied, I just assumed you'd be with a beautiful woman. I wouldn't blame you if you said she was beautiful. She was, Anderson said, but that was years ago. A group of women rushed past Anderson, and he was smacked on the arm with a purse. This sale—it's a zoo in here, he said. The lonely people shop during the week, said Mia. Anderson reached his hand to her waist. A woman like you shouldn't be lonely, he said. Mia didn't answer, and Anderson backed away. I have to go, he said. My afternoon is errand after errand. The barber, groceries, I need an air pump. It's my day off, you know. And behind him the door spun sunlight into the store.

Anderson entered the kitchen where Ermalinda and Claire were sitting at the table in jeans and T-shirts—an open bottle of white wine on the table. Hello, Claire, Anderson said, walking past her. They looked far too much alike, Anderson always thought, though Claire was ten years younger. Hello, Anderson, she said. Ermalinda and Claire continued their conversation, quieter now, though their laughter was loud. Anderson poured a glass of milk and took it to the bedroom. Anderson? Ermalinda called after him. Anderson, are you going to nap? What is it? he shouted. Claire and I want to talk with you. Come sit with us, she yelled.

Anderson left the bedroom for the kitchen where Claire and Ermalinda now had their bare feet up on the table—the yellow light from the window sitting on the green plants as he pulled a chair away from the table, away from their feet. Their wine glasses were stemmed through their fingers; the wine—two still, sunlit pools. Ermalinda and Claire moved onto a new subject: lamps, it turned out, and wouldn't a thin reading lamp be perfect right over there, in the corner next to the bench? The recipe books are right there, and that bench never gets used. I think I'll shave, Anderson said.

Anderson usually shaved in the evening to save time in the morning. When they were first married, Ermalinda used to tease him by saying that she had more body hair than he. Because you're a beast, Anderson thought now to himself as he stood before the bathroom mirror. And in his mind appeared Mia. Hair on her head and nowhere else. At least he didn't think so. He imagined her green panties—his fingers pulling them to the side at the small space between her legs—and he felt himself move closer to the sink, though he looked down at his stationary feet. Anderson had an erection, and he locked the door.

Anderson? Ermalinda called through the door. I'm in the bathroom! he shouted. I know you're in the bathroom, she said. You've been in there a long time, and I've left my book on the stool by the bathtub. Claire has left and I'm going to read. It's by the bed! he yelled. No, she said, not that one. Well, can you wait a minute? he asked. Fine, said Ermalinda, but don't be forever. Anderson stood at the sink with his erection. I won't be forever, he said, and he began to slowly stroke himself. Baby, he said to Mia. Her pouty mouth when he first mentioned Ermalinda. Her bangs. Her Barbie doll hips. And today, looking so pensive, almost regretful in her olive-colored undergarments. Oh Anderson, he could hear her say. He could feel her breasts soften under his touch. Her nipples harden into marbles. And between her legs he felt—Anderson! called Ermalinda. Can't you at least hand it to me? I can't! he said. Go away—just go—I'll be a few—and his voice was sucked from his chest like the escalator steps into the second floor, and he exhaled a long, pulsing breath. Minutes, he said lightly. He leaned forward onto the sink, holding himself up with his left hand. Minutes, he whispered again.

The next morning Anderson found Ermalinda in the living room, asleep in her reading chair. He slid her book through her fingers and almost pushed her hands to her lap, but he didn't want to wake her. He turned and unhooked his bicycle from the wall, then wheeled it into the hallway. He walked it down the two flights of stairs, the back wheel bumping behind him, and he rode it to work instead of taking the train.

He pedaled fast through the quiet streets of Beacon Hill. He coasted down the slope of the Commons, turning his head to the vendors—Boston T-shirts and sweatshirts hanging from a line like laundry. He looked at the people reading on park benches and lying on blankets, and he resumed his pedaling, though he was still riding downhill. On Boylston he sprung from the sidewalk onto the street, and he rode with the traffic to Copley. He weaved around double-parked cars. He thumped the trunk of a taxi when the light turned green. He flipped a man off for turning in front of him, when *he* had the right-of-way. And when he arrived at the department store, sweaty and wrinkled, Julian took his arm. Anderson, he said, what happened? You look like you did somersaults to work. You'll have to buy something from Clearance. Come with me.

Wiping sweat from his forehead with the back of his hand, Anderson followed Julian to the rack of clothes marked down forty percent. This might be nice, said Julian. He held up a summery mint-green pants and shirt set. Oh, what the hell, said Julian, who's going to buy this? Just take it—I'll cancel it out. We sold these to that bus of seniors from Canada. The whole line of 'em. This is the only one left, he said, and he held it up next to Anderson. Yup, just right. He nudged Anderson with his pointer finger. Well, go on, into the fitting room to change.

You look like your own grandfather, Mia said later that morning when Anderson walked up to her. She was wrapped in a pearl-colored robe that stopped just below her panty line. Then I'm a dirty old man standing here next to you, Anderson said shyly, trying to hide his sheepish smile. I used to work in Career Woman, you know, Mia said. A briefcase at my feet and a pen in my breast pocket. They moved me to Lingerie when Sylvia stopped standing straight. They took away my pen and slid red panties up my legs. I'm sorry about yesterday, said Anderson. It's just that with you it's different. Different, repeated Mia. I mean that I like to talk with you, said Anderson. Can you take a walk? he asked. No, Mia said, looking away. But we can talk here.

They were quiet for a moment. Then Mia spoke first. She reads a lot, you said of Ermalinda. Does she ever tell you about it? I mean is that part of your relationship? Anderson sat down on the sales counter. Used to be, he said. Now it's like I said: two beans. Mia tucked her hair behind her ear. I once had someone who read. He still has something that belongs to me, she said. Will you ever get it back? Anderson asked. I don't think so, she said, he's had it for so long. And I'm certain, by now, he's taken it to Gdańsk. There was one night, Mia continued, in our black kitchen when he was speaking beautiful sentences in English, but then he stopped himself and asked me, what is the allure of all this, Mia? He took my hair in his hands, then dropped it. He took my right shoe off my foot and dropped that too. He left after that, and I waited for him all night at the table. But I fell asleep. Never had I been so tired. When I awoke the next morning the apartment was so cold I couldn't move my fingers. How my elbows ached. The plant on the windowsill was glowing—it was horribly green, and I watched it breathe and stretch in the first light.

A Seat
at the
Table

That's her, Rosetta says to Irene, the young widow Mother is always talking about. The girls stare into the café windows across the street. Mother says she sits in the café all day drinking espresso, and when Paolo sweeps the floor each evening, demitasses and saucers are stacked on her table in towers. The girls tie kerchiefs around their heads and continue walking toward the underpass that leads to the market. Mother thinks we should invite her for dinner, says Rosetta, but Father says let her alone—at our table she will feel her mourning a burden. Think how many demitasses she could fit on our table, Irene says to Rosetta. At the market the girls hold hands and squeeze through a labyrinth of fruit, vegetable, and fish stands. Being the youngest,

Irene is handed a pear by a man standing behind piles of green produce: pears, avocados, celery, lettuce, limes. For you this pear is no price, he says. Walking home with wrapped fish and a sack full of Roma tomatoes, Rosetta and Irene pass the pear back and forth, taking bites. Do you think she's still there? Irene asks. Probably, Rosetta says, let's walk by and see. From the underpass they walk three blocks toward the harbor and stand across the street from Caffé Paradiso. I don't see her, Irene says, maybe she's gone. It's only afternoon, Rosetta answers, she won't be gone yet. Father says the cure to a sad heart is a good day's work. This café is her work, Rosetta says. Through the window they watch a young woman sit down, and from behind her a man in an apron sets on the table a small cup and saucer. She's back, Rosetta says, we can go home to Mother now. That evening Rosetta and Irene sit at the dining room table with their mother and father. Mother is talking of the fabric she will use to sew curtains for Nona; Father is eating forkfuls of fish. There's an extra seat, says Irene. She could sit across from Rosetta. Who could sit across from Rosetta? Father asks. The widow, Irene says. We saw her at the café this afternoon. Rosetta looks up from her plate. Irene, says Father, what the widow needs is solitude, and plenty of rest. She will let him go while she sleeps. Father looks at Mother who looks at Irene who looks at her plate. But, Father, Rosetta says, it is just the opposite. She drinks espresso all day so that she will not sleep. Staying awake is like drinking his voice.

Correction

after the drawings of Douglas Miller

———

We'd heard from a friend about the art student at the university whose upcoming show was going to feature portraits he'd drawn of rescue animals. The show was going to take place in an old warehouse downtown. Half the ground floor had been converted into a café, the other half a gallery. The second and third floors had been partitioned into studio spaces, and it was rumored that a famous Columbian sculptor who'd been working on the same bust of his brother for the past seventeen years—starting over again and again—was renting a studio on the third floor.

Eli and I met at the warehouse café an hour before the show on Friday. We'd been having some trouble, and a few weeks prior

I had begun sleeping at my own apartment—something I hadn't done in nearly two years. Eli had come straight from the private high school where he taught violin. He was wearing an ivory dress shirt beneath a rust-colored sweater vest, and a pair of corduroys. I had on an old pair of jeans and a long, beige sweater. It had been weeks since I'd put on makeup or any clothes that weren't loose and comfortable. I was living off a grant to translate into English two books—one novel and one story collection—by a contemporary Bulgarian writer whose works were unknown in the states, and I didn't go anywhere except to walk to the grocery store, to the post office, or for takeout.

"Hi," Eli said, walking to meet me at the counter.

"Hi," I said.

As we ordered—a cappuccino for me and an espresso for him—the horizontal strip of mirror on the wall behind the barista reminded me that I was an inch taller than Eli, a detail that had surprised me each time we stood in front of the bathroom mirror to brush our teeth, but that seemed obvious to me now. Eli paid for our coffees, and we carried them to a small, rectangular table by the window.

The renovation of the café was not yet complete. The steel blue walls were freshly painted but bare. The scuffed hardwood floor was scheduled to be refinished the following Wednesday, and there were fliers on every table stating that the café would be closed for two days. From the middle of the ceiling hung a chandelier that resembled the kind of mobile that would hang in a child's room. Its three metal free-floating arms were suspended by aerial cables, and attached to each end was a frosted, triangular lamp whose combined light filled the space with a soft, moonlike glow.

"Did you get a chance to read the article?" Eli asked me.

"I started it," I said.

"You didn't like it?" he asked.

"I just haven't gotten through the whole thing yet," I said.

Eli sipped his espresso. "You don't have to read it. I just thought that it might interest you."

"It does." Through the window I watched groups of people walking toward the gallery beneath the lightly falling snow.

After we finished our coffees, we stepped through the inside doorway that connected the café to the gallery, and we joined the crowd of people standing before the drawings and sipping from clear plastic cups. "I'll get us some wine," Eli said as we hung our coats on the rolling coat racks near the front door. He headed off toward the table, and I walked up to the first drawing: a horizontal portrait of a large, short-haired dog—maybe a boxer—resting on its hind legs, its front paws outstretched. Its head, one paw, and a bit of its midsection seemed to have been painted over with white paint. The card next to the drawing read: "*Dog 46*, $300.00. Ink, correction fluid, acrylic on paper." I looked again at the drawing. When I examined the space where the head would be I could see only a slight suggestion of its shape beneath the correction fluid.

Eli appeared beside me and handed me a plastic cup filled halfway with white wine. He looked at the drawing and didn't say anything. He sipped his wine, and we moved to the next drawing, "*Dog 23*, $350.00. Ink, correction fluid, acrylic on paper." This vertical drawing portrayed a side view of another large, short-haired dog—this one standing, and leaner than Dog 46. Its body was sketched in a few quick lines, but its head was drawn and shaded in detail. Thick, white correction fluid was painted around the right ear, at the top of its long neck, and above its left eye.

The next drawing, *Dog 12*, which also used correction fluid, showed two attempts at drawing the same bulldog—one sketch directly below the other. The heads were almost identical, save for a slight shift in angle. The lines of the bodies bled into one another, so that at first glance the drawing appeared to represent one dog with two heads.

At the end of the night, as we were approaching the coat rack, Eli touched my elbow. "The mistakes are a part of these drawings," he said.

I didn't respond.

He sifted through the rack for our coats. "Do you want to get a drink somewhere?" he asked.

"No. I need to work more when I get home."

He handed me my red wool coat. "Do you want a ride?"

"Thanks," I said, "but I feel like walking."

Eli buttoned his coat slowly. "I know things have been strained," he said, "but I want you to tell me if you've already given up."

I didn't know what to say, so I didn't say anything. After a minute or two, Eli kissed my cheek, then stepped outside. He walked across the street to his rusty green wagon, and I watched him open the door, get inside, and drive off.

When I could no longer see his car, I left the gallery and began walking in the opposite direction down the partly abandoned street toward my apartment. Every block or so, I passed the windows of a lighted restaurant on the first floor of an otherwise empty building. All sorts of places had begun popping up on this street—a bakery, a small wine shop, an art supply store. My apartment was one neighborhood over, in Butchertown, and I was halfway home when I decided to turn back. I walked briskly through the winter air to the gallery, opened the glass door, and stepped into the yellow warmth of the lights. I headed straight to the wine table and asked the tall woman pouring chardonnay if she could point out the artist to me.

"He's gone," she said. "Is there something I can help you with?"

"I want to buy a drawing."

"Let me take you to Susan."

When I got home to my apartment, I took down the mirror above the mantel and hung *Dog 46* in its place. I stepped back and looked at the contrast of the white correction fluid and the dark shading on the dog's back and the curve of its thigh. I looked at its mismatched paws—one clearly defined, the other hidden beneath the white paint—almost touching in the bottom right corner of the drawing. I looked at the simple, white-pine frame that enclosed the partial existence of this dog.

A few years later I took a job in New York as an editor at a small publishing house that specialized in Eastern European translations. One afternoon when I was walking to the subway after having coffee with a friend in Soho, I passed two artists selling their work on the sidewalk. I stopped at the first table to look at the first artist's abstract cityscapes—at the precise lines and shapes that formed her paintings. Then I crossed the street to look at the next artist's work.

Lying flat on his table was a horizontal mixed-media piece that showed two red parrot heads: the one on the right was detailed and fully shaded; the one on the left had a finished beak and eye, but the head and chest were faintly sketched and only touched with red. Next to the parrots was a vertical drawing of a giraffe. Its head was drawn in detail at the top of the narrow paper; the rest of its body was scarcely rendered—only a few lines gave it the suggestion of a chest and legs. I looked at the signature under the front hoof. I looked at the artist. He was wearing jeans, and a brown zip-up sweater over a flannel shirt. His hair was dark, and it looked as if it would be curly if he didn't keep it so short.

"I bought a drawing of yours a few years ago," I said. "*Dog 46.*"

He didn't respond right away, so I turned my attention to a large drawing of a horse's head—a profile, a spot on the snout looking as if the ink had been partially erased.

"I sold two drawings that night and used the money to help me move here," he said. "Actually it wasn't until the next morning that I sold the other one."

I looked up at him. "To someone who'd been to the show?"

"Yeah."

I took a step back from the table. "Well, it was nice meeting you," I said, slipping my hands into the pockets of my jacket.

"You as well."

As I walked toward the subway I imagined Eli carrying *Dog 23* up the old staircase to his second-floor apartment, then hanging it between the two tall windows of his living room. I pictured him passing the dog's briefly sketched body each morning on his way to the kitchen to make coffee and studying the details of its head as he sat before the drawing in the evenings with a glass of bourbon—the forlorn look in the dog's eyes so vivid despite the surrounding smears of correction fluid. I thought of the article he'd given me to read before the show—about the artist's views of artifice and the absurdity of our desire for perfection.

A few blocks before the station I stepped inside a small French restaurant instead of continuing to the train. It was empty save for the bartender washing glasses and a middle-aged man eating soup at a table in the corner. I took a seat at the bar and ordered a glass of Bordeaux. And when I finished it I ordered another. I spent the rest of the afternoon drinking wine and thinking about Eli, trying to block out the mistake I made in leaving him.

Women

Gina sits at the table in Paolo's mother's kitchen. Behind her on the counter, Paolo's mother is cracking eggs into a tin bowl. When Paolo was a boy, his mother says, he wanted to be a seamstress. Gina looks carefully at her hands. A seamstress, his mother says. He was the only male in the house—what with his grandmother, his aunt, and me. He worked for a while for Rosa—did you know this? He sewed buttons and took measurements for hems. I used to knock on his bedroom door when I needed a pin—can you believe it? A mother asking her son for a pin to fasten her blouse? My mother always told me that he was a sensitive boy. But me—I knew it was my fault. Through the window Gina watches a woman pass by beneath her umbrella. She seems to be hurrying somewhere—her red handbag in her red-gloved hands. Gina gets up from her chair and presses her hands against the window, watching the woman disappear down the street. Paolo's mother pauses at Gina's sudden movement. When she can no longer see the woman, Gina sits down at the table, and Paolo's mother resumes her mixing. Paolo's father liked books and the theatre and his bicycle, she says. Sometimes he would leave after dinner and ride through the neighborhood for hours, coming home after I was long in bed. Not asleep, though—never asleep. And as we lay in bed, he describes what he saw: the couple fighting in the street—She yelling at He for leaning his head too far to watch the woman's skirt part as she walked, the butcher in his bloodstained apron reading the paper on his doorstep, the foghorns rolling off the harbor, and the seagulls scattering like leaves. And women, of course—the beautiful women he'd see smoking in café windows or carrying tomatoes home for dinner. I'd lie there imagining them—these women. Gorgeous women with tailored waists and stiletto heels. Stick-figured women: black lines for hands on their hips—skirts that looked like A's—and my Eddie on a stick-figure bicycle, riding by with his head turned, smoking a stick-figure cigar.

Neighbors

1

Lana rang the doorbell, and she and Finn waited on the neighbors' front porch, Lana holding a bottle of white wine. It was a Friday evening in August, and the buzz of insects in the bushes and trees made the whole Louisville neighborhood sound as if it were vibrating.

"I don't think they're home," Finn said, hands in his pockets. He had combed—even slightly gelled—his wavy, brown hair, but it was starting to frizz in the humidity.

"This porch looks just like ours, doesn't it? And the big window looking into the living room?" Lana straightened her skirt and tucked her hair behind her ear. "But their brick is darker."

The front door opened, and Olivia appeared in a knee-length black-and-white striped dress, her dyed blond hair set in a perfect bob. "Come in, come in. It's wonderful to see you again." She hugged Lana, then reached her hand to Finn. "I'm Olivia."

Finn took her hand. "Pleasure to meet you. I'm Finn."

Inside the foyer, Lana stepped out of one of her heels, but Olivia said, "Please, leave your shoes on."

Lana and Finn followed Olivia through the foyer and around the corner to the dining room, where a rectangular table was spread with a white cloth and set with white dishes, crystal wine glasses, and gleaming silverware. There were two white upholstered chairs on one side of the table and two on the other. No chair at the head or foot.

"We'll have a drink in the garden first," Olivia said. "Just step through those doors, and I'll meet you outside."

Olivia disappeared into the kitchen, and Finn followed Lana around the table and through the sliding glass door that led to a little patio. Lana began walking around the garden, careful not to let her heels puncture the small square of lawn that wasn't taken up by flowers, herbs, or vegetables. Finn stood next to the wrought iron table.

"Would you look at these?" Lana said, bending down to touch the silky, blue petals of a bellflower.

The sliding door opened, and a man stepped out in a pair of creased linen pants, a buttoned, yellow short-sleeved shirt and shiny leather shoes. He had a full head of silvery-gray hair. "I'm Burton," he said to Finn, holding out his hand.

"Nice to meet you, Burt. I'm Finn."

"Burton. Not Burt."

"Excuse me. Nice to meet you, Burton."

Lana turned around and walked toward them. "I'm Lana. Olivia and I met at the market last week."

"So she told me." Burton reached out his hand. "Burton. Welcome to the neighborhood."

Olivia appeared with a silver tray on which sat a martini pitcher, four martini glasses and a rocks glass of large green olives pierced with toothpicks. She set the tray on the table, poured the martinis, and stuck a spear of olives into each glass. Then she handed everyone a drink. "To new neighbors," she said, lifting her glass into the air.

"New neighbors," Lana repeated.

Everyone clinked glasses.

"Delicious," Lana said.

"It's our top-secret recipe," said Olivia. "No, I'm just kidding. It's right out of the bartender's manual."

"You a martini drinker, Finnian?" Burton asked.

"Oh. It's just Finn. It's not short for anything." Finn forced himself to take a sip of his martini. "This isn't usually the drink I order, but it's good. Very—strong-tasting."

"You have a lovely garden," Lana said. "Are those radishes I saw?"

"My third planting this summer. We practically live on radishes at our house. Well, radishes and these." Olivia held up her glass. "I'd better check on dinner."

"Can I help?" Lana asked.

"You could slice the bread if you want. My first sourdough. We'll see if it turned out."

"Ooh. Homemade bread." Lana followed Olivia into the house, and Finn and Burton stood across from each other, the wrought iron table between them.

"So, Finnian. What do you do?"

Finn paused, deciding not to correct him. "I'm a set designer. I just took a job at the Actor's Theatre. That's the main reason for our move here." Finn took another tiny sip of his drink.

"We used to take our daughter there to see *The Nutcracker* every year," Burton said.

"Theatregoers, then."

"Children like plays."

"Yes—yes they do," Finn said, nodding.

"But children grow up."

Finn touched his martini to his upper lip.

Olivia appeared at the door. "Ready when you are."

Burton held out his arm, and Finn stepped inside the dining room, where the table was now laid with a lidded casserole dish, a plate of sausages, a salad, and a basket of bread.

"I just need to pop into the restroom real quick," Finn said.

"Through the living room and take your first right," Olivia said, arranging the salt and pepper shakers on the table.

Finn set his full martini glass behind a vase of zinnias on the built-in white buffet, then left the dining room. Fancy, he thought, walking through the green-and-gold-wallpapered living room with its ivory-colored leather sofa and matching armchair. Gilded mirrors hung on the walls, and a shiny black baby grand piano stood proudly in the far corner.

When he returned, Lana, Olivia, and Burton were seated at the table. Lana and Olivia on one side, Burton on the other, across from Lana. The only chair left was next to Burton. On his right-hand side. The full martini glass that Finn had hidden on the buffet had been moved to his place setting, right next to a full glass of white wine. The other three martini glasses sat empty on the buffet.

"Have a seat, Finnian," Burton said, taking the lid off the casserole dish. "Please," he said to Lana. "Help yourself."

Lana picked up the serving spoon. "Are these vegetables from your garden?"

"They are," Olivia said. "I hope you like ratatouille."

"What a treat." Lana scooped a serving onto her plate, then handed the spoon to Olivia.

"So do you miss Boston, or is Louisville starting to feel like home?" Olivia asked, looking first at Lana, then Finn.

"I'm loving it here so far," Lana said. She stabbed a sausage with the meat fork. "This neighborhood is wonderful. We never have to get into the car. I wasn't expecting that."

"Everything you need is at your fingertips here," Olivia said.

Burton passed the salad to Finn. "What were the other reasons for your move here?"

Finn paused as he took the ceramic bowl.

"You mentioned outside that your job was the main reason," Burton said.

"Oh. Right. Well," Finn said, using the wooden tongs to serve himself some salad, "we were ready for a change."

"And we wanted to move to a place where we could afford a house," Lana said. "A place where we'd get to know our neighbors."

"Burton is on the neighborhood association board," Olivia said, reaching for her wine glass.

"Is that like a neighborhood watch?" Lana asked.

"In some ways," Burton said. He sliced into a piece of sausage. "But the association is more concerned with the social side of things. You know—making sure people get along."

"What a great idea," Lana said.

"It's kind of unique to our neighborhood," said Olivia. "I mean, plenty of neighborhoods have associations, but ours is particularly active. Oh, Finn—you didn't get any ratatouille." She handed him the serving spoon.

"I must have missed it." Finn scooped himself a child's-sized portion.

"Will you be working, Lana?" Olivia asked.

"In the admissions office at U of L. I did the same work in Boston."

"There are a couple of U of L professors in the neighborhood," Olivia said. "Ethan—he lives in the white craftsman a few blocks down—teaches history, and Marta, who lives across the street from him, teaches—English?" Olivia looked at Burton.

"Literature," Burton said.

"What kind of literature?" asked Finn.

Burton shrugged.

"What were the people like who lived in the house before us?" Lana asked.

"They were a young couple," Olivia said. "Thirties. About your age."

"Why did they leave?" Finn took his first tentative bite of the ratatouille. Eating eggplant, he had always thought, must be akin to eating an eel. White, slippery flesh inside the tough, purple skin.

"They divorced." Burton sipped his wine.

"How long have you two been in this house?" Lana asked.

"Twenty-two years," Olivia said, using her knife to slide a piece of zucchini onto the tines of her fork. "It's the only house we've owned. We came from a tiny apartment in Beacon Hill, and I mean tiny. Where did you two live in Boston?"

"Brighton. Right on the border of Brookline," Lana said. "You know—out toward BC?"

"The Chestnut Hill stop on the B line was just outside our door," Finn said as if by reflex, then immediately regretted bringing it—that T stop—up.

"I know exactly where you're talking about. There used to be a laundromat right there—The Missing Sock I think it was called," Olivia said.

"Yes!" Lana exclaimed. "It's still there! That's where we did our laundry."

"Burton and I met at BC," Olivia said. "Did I mention that at the market?"

"You did," Lana said.

"And now our daughter is at Brown," Burton said, "studying law. So we get back to New England quite often."

"She's always been Daddy's little girl." Olivia turned to Finn. "Burton's an attorney."

"Oh." Finn took a small sip of wine. "Is your daughter the piano player?"

"No one plays that piano," Olivia said. "I just always wanted a living room with a piano. That was one of the main reasons *I* wanted a house. A piano would have taken up our entire apartment in Boston."

"We couldn't have afforded a house in Boston then," Burton said, implying that they could now.

"Burton and I are from Louisville originally. We moved back after Burton had completed his law degree at Harvard and when I was pregnant with Camille. It was perfect timing, actually. Burton's father was retiring, and Burton took over the firm."

When they had finished eating, Olivia began clearing the dishes, and Burton walked over to the glass-front cupboards hanging above the buffet. He took out four cordial glasses, set them on the buffet, then left for the kitchen, coming back with a chilled bottle of Vin Santo. He filled the glasses and set one next to Lana's empty white wine glass. Finn's eyes widened as Burton set a glass next to his half-full wine glass, which sat next to his full martini glass. Then Burton set down a glass for Olivia, and along with the bottle, he carried the last glass to his seat.

Olivia appeared with forks and a pile of small plates, which she set on the table. Then she returned to the kitchen and came back with a pie.

"Don't tell me you baked a pie," Lana said.

"No. I cheated on the dessert. It's from the bakery up the road. Tina's. You'll get to know it." Olivia set the pie in the middle of the table and began serving everyone a piece. "Lemon meringue."

"Just a sliver for me," Finn said.

"You don't like meringue?" Olivia asked.

"I do," Finn lied. "But I'm pretty full."

"And you've got your work cut out for you there," Burton said, nodding toward the lineup of Finn's martini and wine glasses.

"Well? Should we have another toast?" Olivia said when she'd finished serving the pie.

The four of them lifted their cordial glasses.

"To a lovely evening," Olivia said.

"A very lovely evening," Lana said, and once again they all clinked glasses.

At the end of the night, the four of them gathered in the foyer beneath the small chandelier. Lana and Olivia hugged. Finn and Burton shook hands.

"We had a wonderful time," Lana said. "We'll have you two over once we find all of our dishes."

Everyone laughed.

"Good night," Burton said, closing the door after Lana and Finn had descended the front porch steps.

"Wasn't that fun?" Lana said as they crossed the moonlit street to their two-story, red-brick house.

"You're joking, right?"

"You didn't have a good time?"

Finn opened the front door and flipped on the cracked dome light above. "We don't exactly have much in common with them."

"What do you mean?" Lana asked, stepping out of her shoes. She turned on a lamp in the box-filled living room on her way to the kitchen.

Finn followed her. "For one thing, they're much older than we are."

"And the other thing?"

"They're in a different tax bracket."

Lana took a glass from the cupboard and poured herself some water. "So?"

"They bought a grand piano for decoration."

Lana didn't respond.

"And Burton—what kind of name is Burton?—was pressuring me. Setting another drink in front of me when I'd barely touched the one I had."

"He was just being polite. The host of a dinner party should always make sure your glass is full. How was he supposed to know that you don't really drink if you don't tell him?"

Finn opened the refrigerator and poured himself a glass of milk. "I'm going to bed." He kissed Lana perfunctorily on the cheek.

2

That night Finn awoke to the sound of animals fighting, and he lay in bed listening to the shrill screeching and the patter of footsteps running back and forth on the roof. He lay in bed awake, his mind returning to that evening in Boston—where it always went in the middle of the night when he couldn't sleep. Lana walking into their apartment without taking off her rain boots. Sitting down at the kitchen table. Her raincoat still buttoned. Finn had been at the stove, stirring rice.

"A man asked me out for coffee," she'd said. No hello, no sorry I'm late, no it took forever to catch a train. Her hands were under the table, folded in her lap.

Finn turned around to face her.

"I had one cup. Then I got up and left."

It took a moment—more than a moment—for Finn to speak. "What man? Someone you know?"

"I see him every morning at the T stop. He lives somewhere in the neighborhood."

Their apartment—the third floor of an old house—had been in the Cleveland Circle area, where one can catch the B, C, or D trains of the green line. Finn always took the D line, the fastest train with the fewest stops, getting off at Park Street and switching to the red line, which carried him across the river to the small theatre in Cambridge where he worked. Lana rode the B line—the slowest train with the most stops—as it stopped directly in front of the admissions office.

"This was the only time. I won't see him again. I'm going to start riding the D line in with you. I'll walk from Kenmore."

Steam had stopped rising from beneath the lid, as all the water had evaporated. The rice was now sticking to the bottom of the pot.

"Do you—want to see him again?"

Lana leaned forward, as if she felt sick. "No."

Ironically, Lana's meeting the man for coffee had actually brought her and Finn closer. They began walking to the train together in the mornings, and when there weren't two seats next to each other, they stood close, Lana's arms wrapped around Finn's waist as he held the bar above their heads. They started cooking breakfast together on Saturday mornings and reading aloud in the evenings while sipping lemon tea. But even so, Finn couldn't keep himself from wondering every time he was out in the neighborhood—is that him—the guy in the wool hat, buying a newspaper from the box? Or the muscular man walking toward him with headphones in his ears? Or him—the tall man stepping off the train and disappearing down the street?

Finn got out of bed to try to catch a glimpse of what he figured were raccoons, but all he saw were the streetlamps, the low-hanging crescent of moon, and a lamplit window upstairs in the house across the street. He reached for his glasses on the nightstand, and putting them on, he saw through the window an apricot-colored room, a mahogany desk, a green-shaded floor lamp, then the profile of a man, which suddenly turned and became Burton's face, staring at him. Finn quickly stepped to the side, where he waited, his heart pounding. A moment later, when he peeked from the corner of the window, the light across the street was off. *He couldn't see me, could he?* Finn thought. *You can't see into a pitch-black room from across the street. Can you?*

In the morning when Finn awoke, Lana was not in bed beside him. He looked at the clock on the nightstand. It was ten thirty-seven. He never slept this late. Pulling on a T-shirt as he walked down the creaking wooden stairs, he smelled coffee and heard the radio playing classical music.

Lana was in the living room, unpacking boxes—the sun pouring through the curtainless windows. "What do you think we should do with these shelves?" she asked, gesturing toward the white, built-in bookshelves on either side of the fireplace. "Are we putting all the books upstairs in the study?"

"Good morning," Finn said. He kissed Lana on the cheek, then walked into the kitchen and poured himself a cup of coffee. When he came back he cleared a place to sit on the worn, green sofa. "I liked how we had it in the apartment—books in every room, separated by genre."

"In the apartment we didn't have the option of putting all the books in one room."

"Still, I liked the system we had. I like having books throughout the house. I always find it strange when people don't have books in their homes. Like the neighbors. I didn't see a single book anywhere."

"Most people don't have books in the foyer or in the dining room," Lana said, reaching for her coffee mug on an unopened box.

"We did."

"We didn't have a choice. Anyway, we have the study with all those built-in shelves upstairs. We can put most, if not all, of the books up there."

"Let's at least keep the art books down here."

"All right." Lana found one of the boxes marked "Art Books," and she opened it with the pocket knife that she took from the windowsill.

"Did you hear those raccoons last night?" Finn asked.

"No. I didn't wake up once."

"Well, there were at least two of them—maybe three—fighting on the roof. When I got up to see if I could scare them away, I saw a light on across the street."

"Uh huh?" Lana said, half-listening as she lined up the books on the shelves.

"Then I saw Burton—looking into our bedroom window."

"Sure you did."

"I'm serious. A lamp was on, and at first I just saw a man's profile. But when he turned to face me I saw that it was Burton."

"If you did see him, I'm sure that he was looking at the stars or chasing away his own raccoons."

"No, Lana, he was looking right at me. I'm sure of it."

"Did you have a light on?"

"No."

"Then there's no way he could have seen you." She took the last handful of books from the box and set them on the shelf. Then she opened another box.

"I know what I saw."

Lana didn't respond. She continued stacking books on the shelves. "I was thinking we could walk to the hardware store to get some new stovetop rings," she said. "I don't want to try cleaning the ones we have now. We also need a step stool or something. I can't reach the top shelves of the cupboards. Maybe we can get some breakfast first."

"All right," Finn said. "I'll brush my teeth after I finish this cup."

When Finn came downstairs, Lana was sitting on the sofa, talking on the phone to her mother, so he cut open a box labeled "Small Sculptures" and began arranging them on the mantel. When he was finished and Lana was still talking to her mother, he asked in a whisper if he should just go to the hardware store.

Lana nodded yes. Then she put her hand over the phone and said, "Bring home bread and scones."

At the hardware store around the corner and three blocks up, Finn bought four new stovetop rings and a metal step stool. Then he crossed the side street and walked up the cement steps to the bakery, passing the handful of umbrella'd tables where people were sitting with their coffees, muffins, and scones, reading newspapers or talking. A dog was asleep under the table closest to the door—some kind of Australian sheep dog, Finn thought, though he didn't know much about animals. Just before he looked away, he saw that the dog was missing one of its hind legs.

Inside, Finn took his place in line, looking at the breads on the metal racks behind the counter. When it was his turn to order, he asked for a loaf of cinnamon raisin and a half-loaf of seeded rye. Then he looked in the glass case beneath the register and chose two black currant scones. As he was walking toward the door with his brown paper bag, he heard his name, then saw Olivia standing in line.

"I see you've found the bakery," she said.

"I have. Is this where you got that delicious pie?"

"No, that's Tina's. It's a half mile or so up the road. Right next to a little antique shop. She doesn't make bread. Just desserts."

"We'll have to check it out."

"Once you do, you'll be there twice a week."

Finn patted his stomach, and they both laughed.

"Been to the hardware store?" she asked, looking at the step stool hooked onto his arm.

"We're slowly putting the house together," Finn said.

"Well, Burton and I just had a wonderful time last night."

"So did we. Thanks again for having us."

"We'll do it again. Give Lana a hug for me."

"I will," Finn said. Then he walked out the propped-open glass door.

The sleeping dog was gone along with its owners, and Finn saw that Burton had taken their place. Before giving himself the option to walk by, pretending that he didn't see him, Finn stopped at the table. "Morning," he said.

Burton looked up from his newspaper at Finn, then immediately looked back down.

Finn stood there awkwardly for a moment before quickly continuing to the steps that led to the sidewalk below. On the walk home, he replayed the exchange, or lack of an exchange, in his mind, trying to discern whether he could have missed a nod, a wave, or a whispered hello. But he had been standing two feet away from Burton. It would have been impossible for him to have missed anything.

When he walked into the house, Lana was in the kitchen, scrambling eggs. "That looks perfect," she said when she saw the step stool. "Just set it over there, next to the refrigerator."

Finn slid a stack of boxes out of the way, then leaned the folded step stool against the wall. He set the two bags on the red table pushed against the window that overlooked the backyard.

"You got the rings?"

"And the bread and scones."

Lana poured the eggs into the hot frying pan, and Finn began slicing and toasting the bread.

"I saw Olivia at the bakery."

"Did you?"

"She was standing in line when I was walking out. She sends a hug."

"I really like her," Lana said, pushing a spatula through the eggs.

"And I saw Burton on my way out, sitting at one of those outdoor tables."

"Uh huh?" Lana turned down the flame on the stove.

"I said hello and he ignored me."

Lana sighed.

"I'm serious, Lana. I stopped at his table and said good morning. He looked up from his newspaper—directly at me—then back down at the paper without nodding or saying a word."

"Maybe he didn't recognize you."

"I spent three hours at his house last night." The toast popped up, and Finn put it on a plate, then dropped in two more slices of bread.

"I don't know what to say, Finn. I had a nice time last night, and I really like Olivia. It would make me happy if you got along with Burton. Besides, they're a prominent couple in the neighborhood. They'll help us get to know other people."

"I said good morning to him, didn't I? He's the one who ignored me. Why don't you believe me?"

"I do. Okay? I do believe you. I just think that there might be more to the story—something you might have missed."

"You can think that if you want to, but I was there, and I know for a fact that there was nothing to miss."

Lana divided the eggs between two plates, then carried the plates to the table. She took forks from the drawer and glasses from the cupboard. Then she grabbed the carton of orange juice from the refrigerator. "Can we stop with the Burton suspicions? I'd really like to enjoy my breakfast. And the day."

"Okay, but they're not suspicions." Finn carried the plate of toast to the table along with the dish of butter and two knives. He sat down across from Lana and began buttering a slice of rye.

"My mom is going on a singles cruise," Lana said.

"Where?"

"The Caribbean. In October." Lana poured herself some juice. "I'm not sure how I feel about it. My father hasn't even been gone a year."

"She's lonely, Lana. What do you expect her to do? Sit in her house all day and knit? Your mother's a very social person."

Lana took a bite of toast and stared out the window.

"She's also very picky," Finn said. "I wouldn't worry too much about her bringing someone home."

Finn and Lana spent the afternoon unpacking boxes—Finn in the study, Lana resuming her work in the living room. By late evening, the living room was finished, save for washing the floor and hanging the curtains that they hadn't yet bought. There was still a stack of boxes in the study. For dinner, Lana walked to the Indian restaurant where she'd placed an order. When she got home she opened a bottle of Perrier, and they ate on the front porch—at the teak table and chairs that the previous owners had left behind, as if they were in too much of a hurry to get out.

After dinner they made a yellow cake from a mix they'd found in the box marked "Food" that had been hidden in the foyer beneath a pile of coats, and in the same box they'd found a small container of chocolate frosting. They ate the cake with glasses of milk on the sofa, looking around at their new living room.

"You did a nice job in here," Finn said. "But it still feels a little bare."

Lana licked her fork. "We need another chair. Or a love seat."

At midnight, when Finn walked into the bedroom after brushing his teeth, Lana was lying on the bed in the lamplight, wearing a black see-through negligee. Finn climbed onto the bed beside her and put his hand on the curve of her breast. She lifted her head to kiss him, and he climbed on top of her, holding his weight with his left arm. As he kissed her, he took his hand from her breast to turn off the lamp, but he couldn't find the switch. He had to stop kissing her to see what he was doing, and right as the bedroom went dark, he saw the lamplit room across the street—the rest of the house was unlit—and he became distracted. Lana pulled at his boxers, but Finn was searching the room across the street. And when she put her hand on him, he was only half hard.

"What's going on?" she asked.

"Nothing."

"What are you looking at?"

Finn scanned the room once more before sliding back onto Lana. He started kissing her again, moving his lips from her mouth to her neck, down between her breasts, and onto her left nipple, erect beneath the silky fabric, but he couldn't focus. He kept feeling that Burton was watching—spying on him as he made love to his wife.

Lana again reached her hand to Finn, but he was soft. She pushed herself up and sat against the headboard. "What is it," she said, sounding hurt, angry, and self-conscious all at once.

Finn sat up near the foot of the bed. "I keep feeling like he's watching."

"Like who is watching?"

Finn didn't answer.

"Oh, you've got to be kidding me. Burton again?" She turned on the lamp and got out of bed. She grabbed her robe from the wicker chair, flicked on the hallway light, and stomped down the stairs.

3

Finn was asleep when Lana came back to bed, and he didn't wake until the next morning when the bells of the Presbyterian church began ringing a few blocks away. Lana stretched and groaned, pulling her pillow over her face. "Make them stop," she mumbled, and Finn closed the windows.

Downstairs he turned on the radio and ground beans to make coffee. As he was filling the glass pot with water, the piano concerto ended and the host came on, announcing a concert that was to take place the following Sunday. A string quartet from Germany was touring the states, and they were going to be playing Mozart's Haydn Quartets in a free concert on the riverfront. Finn wrote down the time and date on the back of a receipt and stuck it with a magnet to the refrigerator.

When the coffee was ready, he carried a cup to the living room, stopping first at the front door to retrieve the Sunday Edition of the *New York Times* before settling down on the sofa. As usual he turned to the theatre section and began reading about the plays that had opened.

Who's Afraid of Virginia Woolf had returned to Broadway, and the show was given a spectacular review. An Off-Broadway theatre was putting on Pinter's *The Betrayal*, and according to the reviewer, the production, while not the best he'd seen of the play, was worth the $85.00 ticket if only for the chance to see the classic on stage. The third review Finn read described a play that followed the course of an affair between two veterinarians. They would meet early in the morning for coffee, then have sex in the exam rooms in the late afternoon, after everyone else had gone. The review had more bad to say about the play than good, but it prompted Finn to wonder, as he often did, what Lana and the man had talked about over the cup of coffee that they'd shared. On a number of occasions he had almost asked Lana, but despite how badly he wanted to know, he knew that it would only make things worse. Besides, the conversation itself wasn't the problem. The temptation never would have come about had the man not been standing next to Lana every morning while she waited for the train.

A half-hour later when Lana came downstairs in her robe, she sat beside Finn on the couch.

"There's coffee," Finn said.

She yawned.

"Should I get you some?" Finn reached for his cup and got up. When he came back, two steaming cups of black coffee in his hands, Lana was reading the obituaries. "I don't know why you read those things." He handed her the chipped, blue mug.

"I found out about Mr. Rothschild from the obituaries in *The Globe*. If I hadn't read them that day, I would still be sending him Christmas cards."

"It's a good thing you stopped," Finn said, sitting down beside her. "He was Jewish."

"His wife was Christian. Before she died—which I also found out from the obituaries—they celebrated both Christian and Jewish holidays."

Finn rummaged through the scattered newspaper on the sofa to find the review he'd been reading. "I heard about a free concert on the radio. A string quartet on the riverfront."

"When?"

"Next weekend. Seven o'clock Sunday night. It might be fun to go."

"All right."

Finn lowered his newspaper. "Why do you sound hesitant?"

"Well, I think it might be nice if we invited Olivia and Burton."

Finn sipped his coffee, burning the roof of his mouth.

"I think it would be more enjoyable for you than having them over for dinner," Lana said. "Besides, the house isn't ready for company. And if we invite them to the concert I won't feel like it's taking us too long to initiate plans."

"You think they're over there counting the days?"

"I just think there's a two-week window during which we should invite them to do something."

"Two weeks? Where did you get this number from?"

"I don't know—I read it somewhere. If we wait too long, they'll assume we don't want a friendship with them."

Finn was quiet.

"We do want a friendship with them, don't we?" Lana asked, running her hand up Finn's thigh and nuzzling her nose into his neck.

Finn set down his coffee, and Lana climbed on top of him, taking off her robe. She was wearing the negligee that she'd had on the night before.

"We don't have curtains," Finn said distractedly, cupping her breast.

"People are either asleep or at church." Lana pulled off his T-shirt and helped him slide his underwear down his legs. Then they made love on the sofa, lying on the scattered newspaper and following it to the floor.

Afterwards, they assessed the damage: one cup of spilled coffee—most of it on the newspaper—and one cracked mug. Then Finn made French toast with the rest of the cinnamon raisin bread, and they ate it at the kitchen table, a warm breeze filtering through the window.

"Fall is already on its way. I can smell it," Lana said, licking the syrup from her finger. "What time did you say that concert was next Sunday?"

"Seven. Do you want this?" Finn pointed at the last piece of French toast on the plate.

"You have it. I'm stuffed." Lana kissed him on the cheek and began clearing dishes. "So you don't mind if I call Olivia?"

"About what?"

"The concert."

Finn cut into the French toast with his fork.

"Finn?"

"No. Go ahead."

4

As Finn had expected, Burton and Olivia accepted Lana's invitation for the following Sunday. The four of them were to meet at the pavilion at six forty-five. At least they weren't driving together.

At a few minutes before six, Lana came downstairs in a summery yellow dress that tied behind her neck, a white sweater draped over her arm. "Are you ready?" she asked Finn, who was half asleep on the couch.

"What time is it?"

"Six. Almost time to go."

"I just have to change and have a quick shave."

"There's traffic in this city too, you know." Lana searched through the hall closet until she found the white sandals she was looking for.

"I'll be ready in ten," Finn said. He was halfway up the stairs.

Lana was in the driver's seat, windows rolled down, when Finn stepped outside.

He walked to the curb where the car was parked. "I can't find my keys to lock the door."

Lana sighed as she turned off the car. She handed Finn her keys through the window.

When he got into the car, she pulled out into the street and headed west toward the riverfront. "You look nice," she said. "I love that shirt on you."

"You picked it out."

"I did a good job." At a red light, Lana reached over and ran her fingers down the buttons of Finn's turquoise, short-sleeved shirt. "But I think these pants have had it."

Finn looked down at the white paint spots on his knees. "I didn't notice."

All the street parking was taken on West Main, so they found a spot in the parking garage near the science museum and walked from there, following the crowd of people past the cast iron facades of the buildings and toward the waterfront.

"Olivia suggested we go out after the concert for a glass of wine."

"Looking forward to it," Finn said.

"Please don't be sarcastic."

"Sorry."

They followed the walkway between buildings to the riverfront park.

"There's the pavilion," Lana said, pointing to the temporary, orange structure erected for summer concerts. "I guess we should just hang around there until we see them."

On the other side of the pavilion Finn could see the Ohio River, murky and barely moving.

"We should have brought chairs," Lana said, looking around at all the people sitting in chairs or on blankets in the grass, waiting for the concert to start.

They walked to the pavilion and stood in the crowd of people.

"What time is it?" Lana asked.

"Twenty till."

"They should be here any minute." Lana used her hand like a visor to shield her eyes from the sun. "Do you see them?"

"Nope."

"You're not even looking."

"It will be easier for them to spot us."

"Why?" Lana asked, irritated.

"Because we're standing still."

"There they are." Lana began waving her arm frantically above her head. "Olivia!" she shouted. "Hold our spot," she said to Finn. "I'll go get them."

Finn watched as Lana made her way through the crowd, turning sideways to slip between people holding plastic cups. She and Olivia hugged, and for a moment Lana disappeared behind Olivia's enormous white sunhat. Then Burton leaned forward and gave Lana a hug as well, his right hand very low on her back—on her tailbone—right where the zipper of her dress began. And when he released her, Finn saw his hand swipe her behind—first one cheek, then the other. "You son of a bitch," Finn said under his breath. "You voyeuristic son of a bitch."

Lana looked for Finn in the crowd, then waved him over. He walked toward them, bumping into people along the way without excusing himself.

"Finnian," Burton said, holding out his hand, the hand that had brushed Lana's ass.

Finn stood with his hands at his sides until Lana nudged him. Then he reached his hand to Burton's, squeezing it just a little too hard.

"Quite a grip you've got there," Burton said jovially.

"Hello, Finn." Olivia gave him a little wave.

Finn nodded.

"Well, there's a tent over there with beer and wine," Olivia said, gesturing to her left. "And we set up four chairs right over there." She pointed toward the crowd of people in front of the pavilion.

"Chairs!" Lana said. "We were just lamenting the fact that we didn't think to bring any. Weren't we?" she said, turning to Finn.

But Finn didn't hear her. He was looking at Burton. "Nice to see you at the bakery the other day."

Lana grabbed his elbow.

"That's the beauty of the neighborhood," Burton said. "You're never alone."

"It's true," Olivia said. "The neighborhood is really like a small town."

"Why don't we get the drinks, Finnian. The girls can make sure our seats don't run off on us."

"Sure, Burt," Finn said, his voice cartoonishly enthusiastic.

Lana stepped on his foot. "I wasn't sure they'd sell drinks here."

"You're in Louisville, honey," Olivia said. "You can buy a drink in church."

"Shall we?" Burton said to Finn.

"Let's do it." Finn slapped Burton on the back.

Lana stood motionless as Burton and Finn walked toward the tent.

"I'll lead the way," Olivia said, and Lana followed her through the crowd.

When Burton and Finn took their place at the end of the line beneath the large, white tent, Burton said, "Looks like this is the line for beer and wine. Liquor is over there." He pointed to the other side of the tent.

"Lana will want white wine. But I'm in the mood for some bourbon."

"Working on becoming a local, eh?" Burton laughed. "I'll join you with the bourbon. Why don't you get the girls some wine, and I'll hop over to the liquor line."

Finn nodded.

"Do you have tickets?" Burton asked.

"The concert is free."

"I mean tickets for buying drinks. They don't take cash."

"No. I didn't—"

"Here," Burton said, pulling out of his pocket a string of connected orange tickets. "We bought plenty."

Finn reluctantly took the tickets, and Burton headed toward the other side of the tent.

Waiting in line, Finn felt like a child whose father had just given him tickets to ride the roller coaster at an amusement park. Someone would have to leave his partner to sit with him—the one lonely kid who fucked it up for everyone else.

When Finn reached the front of the line, he bought two plastic cups of white wine for four tickets each. Burton was waiting for him just outside the tent, holding four plastic cups.

"Thinking ahead," Burton said, lifting two of the cups into the air. He looked at the two cups Finn was holding and said, "The girls can get themselves another. They're bound to need the bathroom at some point, anyway."

Finn followed Burton to the red, portable chairs where Lana and Olivia were sitting, Olivia on one end and Lana next to her. Burton sat down next to Lana. Finn remained standing.

"Finn, honey? There's a seat for you right next to Burton," Lana said in an overly sweet voice.

"I see that," Finn said. He handed the cups to Lana and Olivia, then sat down.

"Thanks, hon," Lana said.

"Yes, thanks, Finn," said Olivia.

"Don't thank me. Thank Burton. Apparently the concert is free, but you need tickets to buy the drinks."

Burton handed Finn two plastic cups of bourbon. "Straight up. Ice just dilutes it."

"There's four ounces of bourbon in each of these cups," Finn said, as if pointing something out to Burton that he didn't know.

"Cheers." Burton tilted a cup toward Finn, then took a big sip.

"I can drive home, honey," Lana said, leaning forward so that she could see Finn.

The crowd grew silent when the musicians appeared through the side door of the pavilion. Two violinists, a violist, and a cellist. Dressed in black, they walked toward the four chairs arranged in a semicircle on the stage. After bowing in unison, they took their seats. Then they lifted their bows to their instruments, and three seconds later began to play.

As Finn listened to the lively first movement of the first quartet, he felt Burton's eyes on him. But every time Finn looked at him, Burton was looking straight ahead.

The crowd began clapping when the movement was over, and the musicians waited impatiently to begin the second—a slower composition, a minuet, in three-quarter time. Finn looked over at Lana—her legs stretched out in front of her, her head tilted to the side. She looked perfectly content sitting there between Olivia and Burton, Finn thought, as if there were nowhere else she'd rather be.

At intermission, Lana and Olivia went to find a restroom, and Finn was relieved when a middle-aged couple came over to talk to Burton. Finn sat there, taking tiny sips—tastes, really—of his bourbon, not actually wanting to be introduced, yet waiting for it nonetheless. But the conversation ended, and the couple said goodbye to Burton and walked away, not seeming to notice Finn at all. Before Finn could ask Burton if they were neighbors, not that he in fact cared, Lana and Olivia were back, fresh cups of wine in their hands.

"Honey," Finn said, looking at Lana. "I thought you said you'd drive home."

"Yes, darling. I did. This is my last glass."

The musicians reappeared and began playing immediately. It seemed to Finn that their playing tonight was a chore and that they just wanted to get it over with. The acoustics were terrible. You had to be right up front to hear well at all, but even that wouldn't make much difference. There needed to be walls and a ceiling for the sound to properly fill the space. And it wasn't like this outdoor venue added much. It was muggy, and the Ohio River was brown and dirty-looking. Finn imagined being on a boat and accidentally falling in, then being pulled back on board covered in muck, a half-dead fish fused to his ankle, trying to suck the life out of him.

When the musicians had finished the last quartet they disappeared through the side door, ignoring the standing ovation from the half-drunk crowd, not wanting, it seemed, to deal with an encore. But they returned to the stage anyway and played one more barely audible piece.

As soon as it was over, Finn stood up and folded his chair, discreetly knocking over his two full cups of bourbon with one of the legs.

"Is everybody up for a glass of wine?" Olivia asked.

"Another time for sure," Finn said quickly, before Lana had a chance to speak. He was the only one standing.

"Not one glass of wine? Or a little something to eat?" Olivia said.

Finn looked dourly at Lana.

"I think we'd better do it another time. Finn has to be at work at six tomorrow morning. Can you imagine?" Lana stood up and folded her chair.

"Storyland starts that early, does it?" Burton said, taking his last sip of bourbon, then sticking the cup inside the empty one in the grass by his feet.

"Just a couple hours before you start fighting to put drunks back on the road."

"Finn," Lana said, shocked.

Burton laughed. "My work is in family law—divorces, mostly. But that's very funny. Putting drunks back on the road."

"Can we help with the chairs?" Lana asked.

"No, no. They're lighter than air. See?" Olivia lifted her chair and swung it over her shoulder. "Let's have coffee this week," she said, giving Lana a hug, then taking her chair.

"I'd love that," Lana said.

"Thanks for the invite." Burton stood up and kissed Lana on the cheek. Then he turned to Finn, reaching out his hand. "Finnian?"

Finn gripped his hand. "Always a pleasure, Burt."

"Burton."

"Right. Burton." Finn handed him his chair.

When Finn and Lana were past the pavilion, Lana said, "Did you really drink both those bourbons?"

"Of course not. I dumped them in the grass. He was mocking me, you know—buying me two bourbons when he knew the most I'd drink was half of one."

"Mocking you by buying you a drink?"

"Two drinks."

They followed the crowd to the sidewalk and toward the parking garage. "I'm driving," Finn said.

"Two glasses of wine for me has less effect than two sips of bourbon for you."

"Are you bragging or putting me down? I can't quite tell."

They drove home—Finn behind the wheel—in silence. He parked along the curb in front of their house and unlocked the front door. Then he followed Lana into the kitchen where she took the open bottle of white wine from the refrigerator and poured herself a glass.

"I think we made a mistake," Finn said.

"What are you talking about?"

"We need to get out of here."

Lana walked out of the kitchen and into the living room.

Finn followed her. "Those people are insane, Lana. Olivia may seem all right, but you can't deny that there's something odd about her. And Burton—a spying divorce lawyer who's head of the neighborhood association? Whatever the fuck that is. I know for a fact that he was watching us the other night—looking into our bedroom window."

"You're the one who's acting insane." Lana sat down on the sofa and turned on the lamp. "And who said he was head, anyway?"

"Of course he is. A guy like that? And it's his job to make sure people get along? Well, what if they don't? What happens then?" Finn stooped down and knelt in front of Lana, putting his hands on the outsides of her thighs. "Listen to me, Lana. I love you, and I have a bad feeling about this place. I need you to trust me on this."

"Please get up off the floor."

Finn stood up. Then he sat down beside Lana.

"I think you should go to bed," she said.

"Well, I think we should talk."

"I don't have the energy to go through this again."

"What do you mean again?"

"There's always someone, Finn. Someone on the doorstep, waiting to intrude on our lives."

"And you're blaming me," Finn said. "It's my fault, isn't it." He stood up and walked toward the stairs. On the first step he stopped and looked over his shoulder. "Don't forget to lock the door."

5

The next day, at the theatre, Finn was working with his crew on the set he'd designed for a 1960s living room. In order to fit the space exactly, they were constructing nearly everything—from the pleated, orange curtains with white, geometric shapes to the walnut-stained stereo console sitting on rounded peg legs. While sanding the surface of an end table, Finn felt at ease, as the entire project was under his control. He had planned every detail—the angles at which the furniture would sit, the placement of each lamp, footstool, and throw pillow. And over the course of the day, he was bothered only by the knowledge that, in a few months' time, he'd have to take the set apart, dismantling his flawless, unmarred world.

When Finn got home that evening at a quarter till six, the front door was open. He entered through the screen door and took off his shoes. He walked through the empty living room to the kitchen, then retraced his steps to the foyer. He called Lana's name as he started upstairs, taking off his paint-splattered shirt and using it to wipe the sweat from his forehead, then his back. In the bedroom he turned on the fan. Then he walked down the hall to the top of the stairs. "Lana?"

He stood there, listening to the quiet of the house and looking at the open front door below. He felt his heartbeat quicken and prickles of sweat begin to form along his hairline. But instead of running down the stairs and out the front door like he wanted to, he forced himself to walk back to the bedroom and into the bathroom, where he ran a cool shower and got in. He closed his eyes, letting the water pummel his face. Unable to clear his mind, he began to imagine Lana talking to Burton in the foyer across the street, Burton's arm outstretched, his hand on the wall behind her head. Then he saw them in the green-and-gold living room: Lana writhing beneath Burton on the ivory leather sofa, Burton's underwear wrapped around his ankles. Finn reached for the soap and began lathering his chest, his underarms, the back of his neck, trying to wash away his anxiety, to rinse off his fear. But when he turned off the water and wiped his face with a towel, Burton was still there—standing over his shoulder, breathing on his skin.

Finn wrapped the towel around his waist and walked through the bedroom and down the hall. He called Lana's name at the top of the stairs, then returned to the bedroom where he rifled through his drawers, throwing clean clothes on the bed. As he was stepping into a pair of boxers, he heard the screen door bang shut, and he raced down the hall. "Lana?"

"Yeah?"

"I'm upstairs!"

"So I gathered." Smiling, she appeared at the bottom of the stairs, holding a cardboard box.

"Where were you?"

"I just ran across the street for a minute."

"For what?"

"Olivia had some vegetables for us. How was work?"

"Fine."

"Only fine? Not good?"

"Good—it was good—everything was fine."

"My day was pretty uneventful too. The usual meetings with prospective students and parents. The air conditioner broke—that was exciting. We had to vote as to which we thought would be better, opening the windows or—"

"Was Burton there?" Finn couldn't hold the question in any longer.

"What?"

"Was Burton there. When you were across the street just now."

"Yes, Finn. That's where he lives."

"I know that's where he lives, I just—"

"You just what? Want to know if Burton and I were alone while Olivia was picking the vegetables? If we'd gone upstairs to his room?"

"No, Lana—" Finn began.

But she was gone. Her bare feet slapping the wooden floor on her way to the kitchen.

Finn returned to the bedroom and finished getting dressed. When he went downstairs, Lana was dicing tomatoes.

"What's that?" he asked, pointing to the frying pan on the stove.

"Okra."

"What do you do with it?"

"What do you think you do with it? You eat it." Lana put down the knife and opened the refrigerator. She took out a bottle of beer.

"I'm sorry," Finn said.

Lana took a sip of her beer, then set it on the counter. She continued dicing the tomatoes. "If you don't want to befriend Burton," she said, "I can accept that. But don't forget that this move was your idea."

"I know. I know it was. I just think we have to go somewhere else. Maybe not to another city, but at least to a different neighborhood."

"There's no escaping," Lana said, pouring more oil into the frying pan. "That man I met for coffee is going to follow us everywhere—to every city, every neighborhood, every house or apartment—until you start trusting me."

Finn was quiet. "I do trust you. I just don't trust other people."

Lana stirred the okra. "That's no way to live. In constant fear that someone is going to swoop in and carry me off—as if I have no choice in the matter. As if what I want and don't want have nothing to do with anything."

"I know."

"I don't think you do, Finn." She stopped stirring and looked at him. "I don't think you believe that I want to be with you—only you—nobody else—and I'm getting tired of trying to convince you. It's—exhausting. Disheartening. I can't keep doing it."

"I believe you. I do."

Lana stood there, looking at him, her hand on her hip, as if she were trying to see behind his eyes—to examine the synapses inside his brain. Then she turned around and reached for the tomatoes, which she dumped into the frying pan. "Will you set the table?" she said.

Finn took dishes from the cupboard and silverware from the drawer and set them on the table. Then he took the iced tea from the refrigerator and poured himself a glass. Lana spooned rice onto each plate and scooped the okra and tomato mixture on top.

They sat down to eat.

"I'll try to make it work here," Finn said quietly, separating the tomatoes from the okra on his plate.

"Our decisions aren't as temporary as they used to be," Lana said. "We own a house now. We can't just pick up and move."

"I know."

Lana sipped her beer. "And I'm tired of feeling like I'm under surveillance. I know that it's my fault you feel threatened, but that cup of coffee was a year and a half ago. You need to get past it."

Finn took a bite of rice. "I will."

After dinner, they read in the living room in front of the fan—Finn a play script and Lana a novel. At ten thirty, Finn closed the script, but Lana wasn't tired.

"I have twenty pages left," she said. "I think I'll try to finish."

Finn stood up, looking at Lana on the sofa. "I meant what I said. I'll get over it."

Lana lifted her eyes from her book. She nodded—a subtle nod, but a nod nonetheless.

Finn kissed her on the forehead, then walked up the stairs and into the bedroom without turning on a light. He didn't turn the light on in the bathroom until he'd closed the door, and he turned it back off before opening it.

He walked through the darkness to the bed, and even though he knew he shouldn't, he peeked across the street through the corner of the window. The living room light was on. So was the porch light. But the room upstairs was dark. He waited for a moment at the window before getting into bed.

He lay first on his back. Then on his side. Eventually he fluffed his pillow and flipped over onto his stomach, where he fell asleep just in time to miss the pull of the chain that turned on the lamp in the room upstairs across the street.

Octaves

At the corner shop in the old Italian neighborhood a woman has come in for an item she forgot to buy last evening. Reading from the stack of newspapers to the side of the register stands a man with a cold. Excuse me, says the woman, for the shop is small, and he must move if she is to get to the aisle she's come in for. Oh—certainly, the man says as he steps aside, patting his nose with a handkerchief. The woman moves into the aisle but is distracted by a box of plum-sized Christmas ornaments. She remembers being a child, stringing her grandmother's tree with beads and hanging red globes just like these. After her grandmother died she was given the ornaments, but she had moved so many times since that she figured she must have accidentally thrown them out. Excuse me, says the man, for he has finished with the newspapers and must pass the woman considering ornaments. Of course, she says, stepping forward. The man, though, stops at a package of polka-dotted handkerchiefs. They look like the handkerchiefs his grandmother would stuff into his grandfather's breast pocket before he'd leave for the train station. His grandfather commuted to the city each morning, where he owned a watch shop. His grandfather, however, never wore a watch. The ticking drives me mad, he used to say. It's five of eight, says the old man with a broom, I am closing in five minutes. The woman with ornaments and man with handkerchiefs turn toward the shelf behind them. They reach their hands for a bar of boxed soap—the only one on the shelf. I'm sorry, the woman says, expecting the man to release his hand from the box. I'm sorry as well, the man says, not letting go. They stand there, the man and the woman, both holding onto the same box of soap. I forgot to buy soap last evening, the woman says, I am completely out. I have no soap, either, the man says—my wife took not only our child but the last bit of soap from our flat. My mother is visiting, says the woman. She's very allergic to cats, and I have three. Without soap to wash her hands, I'm afraid she'll become terribly ill. I have a terrible cold, the man says, and with his free hand he holds his handkerchief in the air for proof. I must wash my hands after each sneeze so as not to spread germs to my daughter, whom I will see on Saturday. She's not yet two—her immune system is so impressionable. My hand is holding more of the box than yours, the woman says. It's the only fair way to decide—you see, I have the better grip. No, says the man. I came into the shop first, meaning my action preceded yours; therefore, the soap is unquestionably mine. The old man sets down his broom. Owning a corner shop, he has lived through too many such disagreements to wait them out. Taking his coat from the coat tree by the door, he leaves the lights and turns the key behind him, locking the voices inside. Outside in the cigar-smoke air he walks down the street of closed storefronts. From an open, second-story window he hears an accordion playing and a door slam shut. His wife, thirty years ago, suitcase in hand—Niccolo, she'd said, I am going to my mother's. I am not a customer in your shop. Our rows resonate in the lower octaves—why don't you hear them?

*Iris
and the
Inevitable
Sorrow,
or
The Knock
at the
Door*

In the oldest part of the city, on a street bustling with foot traffic, a young woman named Iris and her fiancé, Stephen, opened an English-language bookshop so small it gave one the feeling of standing inside a painted telephone booth. The city was cosmopolitan and known for its multilingual readers and so seemed a good place for the American couple to go into business.

One afternoon in February, Iris put on her long, herringbone coat and went to post some mail, leaving Stephen in the window changing the display to Sappho, Euripides, Shakespeare, the Brontës, D. H. Lawrence—writers whose age-old understanding of the interrelation between tragedy and love, of the dependency of one on the other, was sure to sell that month. As she walked past the bookshop Iris waved to Stephen, who, halfway up the ladder, was stringing silver hearts from the ceiling.

A quarter of an hour later when she returned, the shop was locked and Stephen was not inside. A half-dozen hearts dangled above her head—the rest lay lifeless on the top rung of the ladder. On the wooden desk piled with books and papers was a red envelope scribbled with her name. Inside was a card with a small pink heart on the cover, and upon opening it she found in Stephen's handwriting the words, "I've met someone." Underneath his signature he apologized for the misleading card, but Valentines were all he could find in the shop.

When Iris returned home that evening to their third-floor flat in the narrow, three-story building, Stephen's shoes were not on the doormat. His coat was not hanging on the coat tree. His toothbrush was not next to hers in the cup; his shirts weren't hanging in the closet; his socks were missing from his drawer. Iris took off her coat and sat at the table for a long time, which in reality was only a few minutes, but to her it felt like eternity. Then there was a knock at the door. Iris opened it and saw Mirek, the retired chef from the floor below, holding on a silver tray a glass teapot filled with a rose-colored tea and a plate of cold sandwiches. He was surprised to immediately see the young woman's hopeful face, which, upon seeing his, resumed its woe. "You must eat," he said, setting the tray on the kitchen counter. Then he descended the three-dimensional *S* of the staircase.

Because Iris knew the world can do what it wants, she did not linger in her despair. The next morning she unlocked the door of the bookshop and finished hanging the hearts. She spent the week sorting and shelving books, waiting on readers, placing orders, and marking numbers in the ledger. She found herself climbing the ladder with an increased frequency and soon began to miss the ease with which she once handed to Stephen the books whose shelves she could not reach. And because she could not stop the thought that was already on its way, she pictured Stephen's long limbs entwined with another woman's, and from that point forward each day grew twice as long as the last.

On Saturday evening when the week was over and she returned home, there was a note on her door that read, "I invite you for supper this night," and Iris promptly found herself sitting at the kitchen table while Mirek prepared the meal, the back of her chair pressed against the yellow-and-green striped wallpaper. The window to her left overlooked the same art nouveau buildings and sidewalk cafés as her living room window one floor above. The orange trolley car was stopped on the tracks in the middle of the street, and people were climbing up and down its three steep steps.

Mirek's back faced Iris as he worked at the gas stove—the saucepan gurgling, a cloud of fog rising from the pot of water. His body resembled the blocky shape of the stove, and a few stray hairs stood on top of his balding head, shiny with sweat. He carried two plates with meat and dumplings to the table, and they ate in silence, looking up only to sip their wine.

After dinner Mirek fixed coffee on the stove. He poured it into two white cups, set them on saucers, and carried them to the table. "My wife left me many years ago," he said, dropping a sugar cube into his coffee and stirring it with a small spoon. "I was still quite young."

Iris looked up from her cup. "Did she say why?"

"Something would change if she did? No. Nothing." Mirek dropped another sugar cube into his cup. As he stirred, he said, "Being alone is not so terrible. You can have more charge of your life when you are alone. Not complete charge—no one can have that—just more." His spoon made a soft chime when he set it against his saucer. "But first you must stop being in love. This part is not for fun."

A lemony light touched the railing as Iris circled up the staircase. She stopped at the window to look out: the street was empty but for the moon, which, having nothing to do itself, kept surveillance.

Over the next weeks Iris learned to cope, as we all must, with her new circumstances. She pushed herself to get out into the city and to engage with the world. She went to a puppet show, saw three films, and after attending *Madame Butterfly* she dined alone at the new fusion restaurant next to the opera house. Soon she was even sleeping until sunrise without stirring.

Until one night, that is, when she awoke to the faint sound of something springing into the air. She turned on her reading lamp, and there—low in the doorway, perfectly framed in the tunnel of light—was an iridescent brown thing, leggy and skittish. Jumping legs bent, wings angled back, antennae feeling the floor in front of itself. It took one tiny, hesitant step, then another, millimetering itself across the threshold, where it sat, looking at her. Iris reached for the empty glass on the nightstand beside her. She carefully touched her feet to the floor, and the cricket tensed its jumping legs. When she stepped toward it, it leapt into the air and skittered behind the hamper.

They waited each other out until eventually the cricket peeked out from beneath the wicker box. They looked at each other before the cricket disappeared again, reappearing a moment later—scurrying as fast as it could along the wall toward the dresser. From behind the dresser it crept toward the bed, and when she reached for it with the glass, it flung itself at the painting that leaned against the wall—the one of the castle she'd never gotten around to hanging.

She followed the cricket into the living room as it crept beneath bookshelves and behind the armchair, as it scrambled along the telephone cord and underneath the sofa. She chased it as it hopped toward the table, then into the bathroom and under the sink, where it pressed itself against the wall. She waited until it made a run for the toilet—then she slammed the glass down on top of it. At first it didn't move. But when it realized the inevitable, it came to life, flicking itself again and again against the glass.

The clock tower outside her living room window struck six as she put on her robe, exited her flat, and descended the spiral staircase in the cold hallway. She knocked on Mirek's door, and he opened it, a newspaper under his arm. His eyes were alert, but his eyebrows were still asleep. Drooping onto his eyelids, they had not yet begun to stretch out and nestle themselves into their usual entanglements.

"There's a bug," Iris said. "Can you come get it?"

She led him up the winding stairs and into the bathroom. He leaned over, peering into the glass through which the cricket looked out—its compound eyes magnified. "You are of this little guy afraid?" Mirek laughed his husky laugh as he bent down, unrolling his newspaper. "What can he do but jump? Jump! Jump!

What a sad little life." He slid the newspaper under the glass and walked to the door. "I will put him outside."

That evening when she got home from work, Iris hung her coat and satchel on the coat tree and went straight into the bathroom, where she ran a bath in the porcelain tub. The weather had been miserable that day—freezing rain turning into a wet, sloppy snow. She looked into the oval mirror that hung above the sink, pulled her sweater over her head, and unclasped her bra. Slipping the straps off her shoulders she looked at her breasts in the mirror and noticed that one was beginning to droop. The other was firm and proud, determined to defy the deteriorating process that was happening a few inches to its right. She made a cup with her palm and lifted the drooping breast, but when she removed her hand the breast again fell.

After dropping the rest of her clothes into a pile on the floor, she lifted her right foot above the water, touching the surface with her toe and turning her head to look once more in the mirror at her body, or rather, at the body that used to be hers but was now changing into someone else's. Just as she was about to step into the water she heard a quiet sound, as if somewhere very far away two people were walking across a stage in tap-dancing shoes. She covered herself with her hands and looked to her left where the cricket was scampering across the tiled floor. It stopped for a moment, turning its head to look at her before disappearing through the slightly open door. Iris sunk into the bathtub, but she was unable to relax knowing that the creature was somewhere else in her flat.

Later that evening when the teapot was rising toward a boil on the stove, Iris opened the cupboard for the canister of tea and caught the cricket in the light, holding a cracker crumb in its palps. The second it saw her it sprung out of the cupboard and onto the counter. From there it leapt into the air and landed on the floor, stopping for a moment to smooth the tassels of the rug with its front legs before squeezing beneath the door.

The teapot was screeching, but Iris didn't hear it. She was thinking of Stephen, who could never step onto the rug without first straightening its tassels with his toe—of the daily arguments they used to have over those stupid tassels: leaving them versus straightening them or about getting rid of the rug altogether. Iris opened the door slowly. The hallway was empty but for the soft glow of the moon. She waited. Nothing moved. She waited some more. It became clear that she was alone. But as she stepped back to close the door the enormous silhouette of the cricket appeared against the wall. And a few steps below she saw the cricket, sitting perfectly still. When its eyes met hers it hopped down the stairs as fast as it could, taking its shadow with it.

The next evening was Saturday, and the clock tower struck eight as Iris descended the staircase to Mirek's for their weekly dinner. Mirek opened the door in his usual Saturday night bow tie. It was a pleasant red, and tonight he wore it with a blue-collared shirt and a yellow sweater vest that stretched across his stomach. On his lower half were a pair of houndstooth slacks and his beat-up brown slippers. "Good evening," he said, extending his arm to welcome her into his flat.

Iris sat at the table while Mirek opened a bottle of white wine, pouring them each a glass. He set on the table two steaming bowls of borsht, two hardboiled eggs, and a loaf of dark bread. He sat down at the table, dropped a spoonful of sour cream on top of his soup, then handed the dish to Iris.

Iris set the dish beside her and reached for her wine. "Did you ever see your wife again?" she asked. "After she left?"

Mirek buttered a piece of bread. "Her sister came for her things."

"You never ran into her? At a café? Or on the tram?"

"If so I did not know."

"You think she could have changed so much that you wouldn't have recognized her?"

Mirek looked at her with wisdom in his eyes as he reached for an egg, and Iris understood that this meant yes, but that he did not want to call unnecessary attention to her naive question by granting it an answer.

Iris sliced a piece of bread and set it on her plate. "It returned last night."

Mirek squeezed his eyebrows together.

"The cricket," she said.

"Ahh. The same one?"

"It had to be. There aren't many crickets around this time of year."

Mirek dipped his spoon into his soup. Then, as if it had just occurred to him, he said, "There should not be any."

Iris sipped her wine. "When I noticed it, it was looking at me. But not with fear."

"What does this mean *not with fear*?"

"I mean that it seemed to be looking at . . . because I was about to take a . . . and I wasn't wearing any clothes." Iris's cheeks turned pink.

Mirek wiped his mustache with his napkin.

"Then later on, when I was out of the bath, it descended the staircase like a . . . like a person." In one sip Iris finished the wine in her glass.

Neither of them spoke.

Mirek reached for the bottle, but it was light and hollow when he lifted it. He put his hands on his knees to help himself up, when there was a tiny knock on the door.

"Mirek," Iris whispered.

Turning his head to the window Mirek said, "There exists nothing we can do. He will only return again tomorrow. So go. And let him in."

Iris stood up from her chair. The time it took her to walk through the tiny kitchen felt like a year, and by the time she crossed the living room to the front door she felt as if she'd left a long life trailing behind her. She stretched out her arm and twisted the crystal knob. There on the doormat sat Stephen—thorax quivering, one antenna raised in hope.

Silhouette

Inside a small kitchen a woman feels her knees stick to the checkered linoleum floor as she opens a black accordion case. Then, sitting down in a chair, she finds the diamond-studded C base with her left middle finger, and at this small gesture the instrument sighs and gives in to its own song. The man listening to the accordion stands up from his chair and moves to sit at the woman's feet. And there they are: a silhouette for the neighbors to see. Woman in foldout chair with accordion in her lap; man on floor at her feet. The nearby houses (which are broken up into apartments, for this is the old neighborhood, where families used to live) are windows stacked on top of each other, and there are people inside them, looking out. Isn't it beautiful, say the neighbors. It almost looks real—as if she is really a woman and he is a man, and she is playing so that he will listen, and he is listening so that she will always play. A taxicab turns the corner, though none of them leave their windows, for they have nowhere to go as they belong to each other and they are home. The driver, however, honks his horn, and the silhouette changes. One figure stands, and the other stays seated. The accordion is blurred, blending in with the achromatic scene, and the neighbors are unsure as to who has gone and who remains. They hear thunder as figure one or two descends the stairs. The taxi pulls away and the neighbors retreat from their windows, for there is nothing to see once something is gone. Though one neighbor, a meal on his plate at his square kitchen table, keeps his telescope focused on the once-silhouette of two figures. He is waiting while the others have long ago left. Lovers, he knows, are mysterious creatures. One usually opens when the other begins to close. Through his telescope he watched one night, only weeks ago, the man roll onto his back and sigh to the ceiling. The woman shifted her head to lie on his breathing. I was dreaming, he said to her. (This telescope can also magnify a whisper.) In my dream you asked me of the sunflowers that sprouted from the sheets the first night you stayed. And I almost didn't remember, he said. I almost forgot that in the morning when we tried to pick them, their stems were strong as trees.

A
Fulfilling
Life

I was opening a can of sardines for lunch when the telephone rang. It was Carina. I could hear Amadeo and his friends talking and laughing in the background. One of them called out "hey Frenchman" in English, and Carina told him something that sounded like "shut the fuck up." Amadeo and his friends called me "the Frenchman," and being an American, I have no idea why. I asked Carina once, but she never gave me an answer.

"Mac," Carina said into the phone. "Meet me in half an hour. I need to get out of here."

I slid the can of sardines into my refrigerator, then unhooked my circa 1980s celeste green Bianchi from the living room ceiling and carried it down the three flights of stairs. I'd bought it at the flea market when I moved to Salamanca the year before. It has a beat-up white seat and dirty white handlebar tape, both of which I'd meant to replace, but never did. Outside, the thermometer on the stucco building read thirty-four degrees Celsius—too hot to breathe. I rode a few kilometers to the university district and locked my bicycle in front of the sidewalk café where Carina and I most often met. In a red dress and a white wide-brim hat, she was sitting at a small table under an umbrella. I sat down across from her.

"What's going on?" I asked. "You sounded desperate on the phone."

"Nothing," she said. "I just needed somewhere to go. Amadeo has the guys over."

Amadeo, Carina's boyfriend, had been fired three weeks prior from his job at the auto body shop. His friends were over nearly all the time, and at night one of them was usually passed out on the sofa.

"Has he applied for other jobs?" I asked.

"He said he's looking." Carina turned her eyes to the waiter who had appeared at our table.

We each ordered a beer, and I asked her if she wanted to get some food.

"You go ahead," she said. "I'm not hungry."

I ordered a *tortilla de patatas*, then watched the waiter disappear into the dark café.

"How's the book?" Carina asked.

"I wish you wouldn't ask."

"Too late. Tell me what is happening."

I had tried to explain to her that nothing really happens in the book, and that as far as I was concerned plot is for genre writers, but I honestly couldn't tell if she didn't understand what I meant or if she just refused to accept it.

"Well," I said. "Today Nigel made a tuna fish sandwich."

"That's it?"

"I woke up late. Then you called."

"How much are they paying you to write that Nigel made a tuna fish sandwich?"

"Nothing," I said. "At least not until the book is done."

"When you need a job, I'll talk to my department. I can get you some work as a tutor."

Carina teaches English at the University of Salamanca. She's thirty-two years old, short, and beautiful. I have no idea why Amadeo doesn't seem to mind that she spends so much time with me.

"We'll see if it comes to that," I said.

The waiter brought out our beers and a few minutes later my omelette. Carina watched the people walk up and down the narrow street while I ate.

"When is your sister arriving?" I asked.

"Next week. If she's still coming."

"She doesn't want to?" I said with my mouth full.

"We made the plans when Amadeo was still working. I don't want Leda in the apartment with those guys over all the time."

"Can't you tell that to Amadeo?"

Carina looked up at the balconies behind me and sipped her beer. "One of my colleagues is having a party on Saturday—a sort of end-of-the-year get-together. Do you want to go with me?"

"Sure," I said.

"I'll come by your apartment at nine. We'll take a taxi from there."

Carina paid our bill. We took turns, though I'll admit that she paid more often than I did. I think she was worried that I would run out of money and have to go back to the states.

When I got home I sat down at my electric typewriter—another find at the flea market. I had abandoned my dying desktop in Copenhagen and have since succumbed to this flat-looking Olivetti Lettera 36 with its black top, white body, and keys. I turned the platen knob and read the last sentence I had written.

Nigel made a tuna fish sandwich and sat down at the table.

Nigel is a single man in his early forties based in large part on yours truly. He's six feet tall, his hair is beginning to thin, and when he looks into the mirror he sees the memory of strength in his muscles. His girlfriend just broke up with him—imagine that—and he's feeling fat, ugly, and depressed. Nonetheless Carina's right. He's got to do something else today aside from making a tuna fish sandwich. But what gives him the right to a fulfilling life? I got up from my desk and stepped out of the living room and onto the balcony. I listened to a young man below play a couple of sad songs on the violin before putting the instrument away and heading, I assumed, home. It was almost two o'clock. Time for siesta. When he was gone, I watched a yellow lab walk lazily down the street, stopping in the shade of a building to fall asleep himself.

Carina buzzed up to my apartment at a quarter of nine on Saturday evening, and I ran down to let her in. "Want a drink before we go?" I asked.

"All right," she said.

I followed her up the stairs and into the kitchen, where I poured two glasses of sherry. We took the drinks into the living room and sat down on the old sofa that I'd covered with a white sheet.

"Leda is coming on Wednesday," Carina said.

"You talked to Amadeo?"

"I was hoping that she could stay here. With you."

I took a sip before answering. "Here?"

"I know you have your writing to do, but she'll only be around to sleep. She can sleep on the sofa. That's where she'd be sleeping at our place anyway. I know it's a lot to ask, but—"

"It's not," I said, setting my glass on the coffee table. "But I'll sleep on the sofa. She can have my room."

At a quarter of ten we hailed a taxi in front of my building. The party was in the *Garrido Norte* district in a mid-sized flat. The stark white walls and faux leather armchairs reminded me of my place in Copenhagen, except that that apartment was actually my girlfriend's, and much smaller. Or maybe it just felt smaller because it was strewn about with her dirty laundry and terrible drawings. I met more of Carina's colleagues, along with the department chair, who, no matter how many times Carina corrected him, kept referring to me as her boyfriend. She eventually gave up correcting him. At two thirty Carina and I got into a taxi, which stopped first at her place, then at mine.

I woke up at noon with a terrible headache. I took three aspirin, ate some yogurt, and made myself a Nescafé. Then I sat down at the typewriter. Nigel was still stuck at the table with his tuna fish sandwich. Pathetic. I stared at the page until I got the idea to backtrack and lead up to the tuna fish sandwich, and I opened my notebook.

Three scenarios which could result in the tuna fish sandwich:
1. *Nigel wakes up in the middle of the night and can't get back to sleep. He makes a tuna fish sandwich.*
2. *It's lunchtime on Saturday. Nigel considers walking down the street for Vietnamese takeout, but he doesn't want to get stuck talking to Bart, the annoying attorney who eats there everyday for lunch. Then Nigel thinks: It's Saturday—does he eat there on Saturdays? Just in case, Nigel makes a tuna fish sandwich.*
3. *Nigel's ex-girlfriend is coming over "to talk." When she arrives he takes her raincoat and hangs it in the closet. He opens a bottle of wine. He makes a tuna fish sandwich and cuts it in half.*

I'd been writing for barely an hour when the phone rang.

"Leda is coming tomorrow instead of Wednesday," Carina said. "I hope that's all right. She's taking the fifteen forty-five from Madrid."

"Sure," I said.

"We'll drop her things off sometime after eight, then go out for a drink? The three of us?"

"Sounds fine."

After I hung up the phone I immediately began cleaning my apartment. I shook the rugs out over the balcony, then swept and washed the parquet floor. I put new sheets on the bed and moved the books from my nightstand to the living room shelf. I cleaned the bathroom sink and toilet and scrubbed the tub. I did the dishes and threw out the old containers from the refrigerator. By nine thirty I was asleep on the sofa.

The next morning I awoke early to two people arguing in the street, and I couldn't fall back asleep. I carried my bicycle down the stairs and rode to the market, where I bought two kinds of cheese—*manchego* and *hinojosa de duero*, cured ham, a loaf of bread, tomatoes, figs, some Italian coffee beans, a liter of milk, and a bottle of mineral water. It had been a long time since I'd had a woman stay overnight. I loaded everything into the two grocery totes that hung from the rear rack on my bicycle.

At a quarter after eight my buzzer rang, and I jogged down the stairs. Carina, in a long, pink dress, was holding the handle of a suitcase. Leda, taller and thinner than Carina in tight jeans and a white blouse, carried only her purse.

"Bienvenida," I said, kissing Leda on both cheeks, then Carina, though it had been a long time since Carina and I had abided by the tradition. Things had become slightly awkward one time when our lips had accidentally brushed, and we sort of phased out the ritual without either of us acknowledging it. I took the suitcase from Carina and followed the two of them upstairs. Leda's musky perfume filled the stairwell. I carried the suitcase through the living room and set it in the bedroom. Leda was right behind me. "This is where you'll sleep," I said.

"What about you?"

I pointed toward the living room. "On the sofa."

Carina called out that she was opening a bottle of wine.

Leda and I went into the kitchen and took the glasses that Carina had poured. We toasted, took a sip, then walked out onto the balcony. I had only two chairs, but Leda said that, after sitting for nearly three hours on the train, she preferred to stand. The sun had begun its descent, but it was bright enough to make Leda's shirt transparent and to reveal the purple bra beneath it.

We took a taxi to the Plaza Mayor, and by ten o'clock we were sitting at an outdoor table with a ceramic pitcher of Sangria. The square was crowded as usual—half with tourists, half locals. We ordered a few tapas dishes to start while Carina and Leda spoke in Spanish about their parents, their older brother's new wife, and who knows what else. I could follow only half the conversation, but it was a gorgeous night, and I was happy just to be out in it. When the conversation turned to English, Leda asked me what I liked best about living in Spain.

"The late dinners, the siestas," I said. "It's all very different from the way of life I grew up with."

"I can't imagine a day without a siesta," Leda said. Then she said something in Spanish to Carina, and they went off on another tangent.

It's true that after living in Spain it would be very difficult to return to an American life. But then again, the lives I lived in Madison, in St. Paul, in Baltimore, in Toronto, in Copenhagen, and now in Salamanca have all been more or less the same.

At two o'clock Leda and I got into one taxi and Carina another.

I woke up by nine and quietly made a cup of Nescafé. I took the mug along with my notebook onto the balcony and shut the door. It was very warm out, and the sky was hazy, but the slight breeze felt cool against my skin. The sound of motorbikes echoed through the streets below as I began drafting an argument between Nigel and the graduate student who lives in the flat next door. Nigel was finally going to confront him about the smell of garbage in the hall, and if he was feeling confident, the amplification of his sexual delight through the vents.

Leda slid open the balcony door in a loose T-shirt that barely covered her underwear. "Where will I find the coffee?" she asked, rubbing her eyes like a small child.

I set my notebook on the table and got up from the chair. "Good morning," I said, trying not to look at her long, thin legs. "I'll make some."

She followed me into the kitchen and leaned against the counter while I ground the beans and made the coffee in the aluminum pot on the stove. "Do you take milk?" I asked.

She shook her head.

Waiting for the water to boil, I took demitasses and saucers from the cupboard and two small spoons from the drawer. When the coffee gurgled into the upper chamber of the pot I poured it into the cups and handed one to Leda. Then we went out to the chairs on the balcony.

"Did you sleep all right?" I asked.

"Yes. Great." She sipped her coffee. "What were you working on before I interrupted you?"

"Nothing important, unfortunately."

"My sister tells me you're a very good writer."

"We'll see if I can finish a second book."

"What's it about?"

"A man."

"Sounds interesting."

We laughed a little and looked at the building across the street. A man one floor up was leaning over his railing, smoking.

"Carina talks a lot about you," Leda said.

"She and I have become good friends."

We finished our coffees and sat for a while in silence. Leda seemed to me the kind of person who takes a long time to wake up.

Eventually I took the cups inside and made more coffee. I sliced some bread, ham, and cheese, then carried everything out on a tray and set it on the small table.

"What do you think of Amadeo?" I asked Leda, pouring coffee into both cups.

"I've never met him."

I looked at her. "Really? Well, I'll be curious to hear what you think."

"Carina says he's busy, but I don't think he knows I'm here." Leda ate a piece of ham with her fingers. "What do you think of him?"

"Personally I think he's kind of an ass," I said, sitting down. "But a lot of men are at his age. I was."

"How old are you?"

"Older than Amadeo."

Leda smiled.

I ate some bread and cheese. "Your sister will be over this afternoon. I'm not sure what you want to do until then."

"Don't worry about me," she said. "I'll have a shower and go for a walk. You can do your work."

After breakfast I did the dishes while Leda showered. She walked from the bathroom to the bedroom wrapped in one of my towels. Having a woman wearing only a towel in my apartment, even if it was Carina's younger sister, made me feel happy in a way I hadn't felt in quite some time.

I was reading on the couch when she came out in a blue skirt and a yellow shirt with thin straps.

"Do you need directions anywhere?" I asked.

"I'll find my way," she said. Then she leaned over and kissed my cheeks.

When she was gone I sat down at the typewriter and wrote through the tuna fish sandwich that Nigel and his ex-girlfriend were splitting along with a bottle of wine. He was of course hopeful that she wanted to get back together, but it turns out that she was just lonely and wanted to feel desired.

The buzzer rang in the late afternoon, and I went down to open the door. It was Carina.

"I thought you were going to be your sister. I forgot to give her a key."

"She's out?"

"She went for a walk a few hours ago."

We went upstairs and sat down on the sofa. "How are you two doing?" she asked.

"Fine," I said.

"She's not disrupting you too much?"

"Not at all. I'm enjoying the company."

"I was hoping you'd say that. Do you have anything cold to drink? White wine?"

I went to the refrigerator and took out an unopened bottle of Verdejo. I carried it with two glasses and a corkscrew to the living room.

"What are your plans for tonight?" I asked, pouring Carina a glass and handing it to her.

"You're not going to join us?"

"I wasn't sure if you wanted some time alone."

"No," Carina said. "I'd rather you keep us company."

I poured a glass for myself and lifted it into the air. "Salud."

"Salud."

We were on our second glasses when the buzzer rang. Carina went down and came back with Leda, who was carrying three shopping bags. Leda set the bags in the bedroom, then took a seat on the wicker chair across from us.

"Wine?" I asked her.

"Please," she said.

I got a glass from the kitchen, filled it with the last of the wine, and handed it to her. I put some Charles Mingus on the stereo and got a bowl of figs, which I set on the coffee table. Then I opened an Albariño.

Carina asked Leda what she wanted to do tonight.

"I wouldn't mind just hanging around here," she said. "All that shopping made me tired."

We listened to the music and drank the wine. At eight o'clock or so, Carina got up to look in my fridge. Then she called out to Leda in Spanish, and Leda went into the kitchen. The two of them started cooking, and I turned up the music and took my wine onto the balcony.

When Carina called me inside, the table was set with three bowls of chilled cucumber soup and three plates of lettuce with sliced ham, toasted hazelnuts, and shaved *manchego*. There was a basket of sliced bread and a bowl of olives. As soon as we sat down to eat, Carina's phone rang, and she got up to answer it. She took it onto the balcony and closed the door behind her.

"This soup is delicious," I said to Leda.

"It's our mother's recipe."

"Well, you really pulled it off."

"Carina made it. I'm not much of a cook."

Carina slipped back inside, sitting down at the table as if she'd never left, but she was noticeably quiet.

"I was just telling Leda that the soup is delicious," I said to Carina.

She forced a smile.

Leda said something more about the soup in Spanish, holding her spoon in the air. And after tasting the soup herself, Carina seemed to agree.

When we had finished eating, I brought out a bottle of cognac. Carina changed the music, and she and Leda tried to teach me to do the *fandango*.

Carina left at one, and Leda and I took our drinks out onto the balcony.

"I'm surprised that you and I haven't met before," I said.

"Carina and I are in and out of touch."

A red Fiat drove by below, blaring terrible pop-rock.

"Really? I thought you two were pretty close."

"We live in different cities, have our own lives." Leda sipped her cognac. "We had a sister between us—two years older than me and three years younger than Carina. She died when she was sixteen. Carina probably didn't tell you."

"No," I said. "I didn't know."

"Carina feels obligated to have a relationship with me because we don't have Nela."

"She's told you this?"

"Of course not." Leda stepped into the apartment and came out with a pack of cigarettes and an empty glass. "Do you mind?"

I shook my head.

She lit a cigarette, inhaled, then sat back down. "What about you? Who's in your life?"

"I have a brother in the states. I see him every couple of years or so. My parents are both gone."

"Ever been married?"

"No."

A taxi stopped across the street and sat along the curb.

"Do you have a boyfriend in Madrid?" I asked.

"A girlfriend, actually. Ines." She tapped the cigarette on the edge of the empty glass.

"Has Carina—"

"No. Just as I haven't met Amadeo."

When Leda finished her cigarette it was almost two o'clock.

"We should get some sleep," I said.

I carried the glasses to the sink, and Leda brushed her teeth in the bathroom. When she came out, I was spreading a blanket over the sofa.

"Have you ever—" She paused for a moment. Then she walked to the bedroom and leaned against the doorway. "I mean, let's say there's no Amadeo."

"She's been with Amadeo ever since I've known her." I let the blanket fall from my fingers. "I've never had the chance."

Leda looked as if she were about to say something more but decided against it. "Goodnight, Mac," she said, and closed the door.

At nine o'clock the next evening the three of us took a taxi to a restaurant that serves typical Castilian food in the *Garrido Sur* district. It's a swanky place—red walls, rectangular tables with white cloths, a couple of modern chandeliers. We were seated in the back of the restaurant, near the kitchen, and it was very hot. Carina ordered a Rioja, and we drank it while looking at our menus.

"Do you dine out much in Madrid?" I asked Leda.

"Yes," she said. "But at cheaper places than this. Carina is spoiling me."

I smiled at Carina, but she was looking across the restaurant in a sort of daze.

"The suckling pig here is wonderful," I said. "I think that's what I'm going to have."

Our bottle of wine was empty by the time the waiter returned, and we ordered another along with our meals. Chorizo and potatoes for Leda, garlic prawns for Carina, and the roasted pig for me.

"Are you excited for the summer break?" Leda asked Carina.

"I'll miss working with my students. The university isn't offering a course."

"Carina was always the smart one," Leda said to me. "When I was a student I couldn't wait for school to let out."

"I was too studious," Carina said. "Leda has always been more fun to be around."

Leda was leaving in the morning, and it became clear to me that they were already starting to miss one another, or perhaps to miss the relationship that they wished they had.

The waiter brought out some bread and olive oil. Leda took a piece of bread and passed the basket to Carina, who handed it to me without taking a slice. She poured herself more wine.

"Amadeo and I are getting married," she said.

Leda and I looked at her.

"Congratulations," Leda said.

I was quiet.

"I'll have to come back soon to meet him," Leda said, even though it was clear to all of us that she was just being polite.

"When is the wedding?" I asked.

"I don't know exactly. But soon. We want to start a family and—"

"Amadeo wants to start a family?" I interrupted.

Leda and Carina looked at me.

"I'm sorry. I just never pictured him as a family man."

"You hardly know him," Carina said, a tinge of bitterness in her voice.

"I think it can be hard to picture someone with children when you're used to him without," Leda said.

"Does he even have a job?" I asked.

"And what kind of job do you have?" Carina said.

"If someone were relying on me, I'd have some incentive to work harder."

The waiter brought out our meals. He set them before us, then refilled our water glasses with a pitcher. Every couple of minutes the kitchen door swung open, blowing over us the hot, sticky scent of roasted meat. Waiters rushed by with trays of food and busboys with dirty dishes. A man with a guitar appeared on a stool in the middle of the restaurant. He began playing what people outside of Spain refer to as "Spanish guitar." We ate almost the whole meal in silence.

"I think we just have to do the best that we can," Carina said without looking up from her plate. "With work and with love."

"I agree," Leda said.

I sipped my wine.

Before parting with Carina, we made plans for the morning. She would come to my place at eleven for breakfast, then go with Leda to the station. After seeing Carina into a taxi, Leda and I went for drinks at a bar with live electropop a few blocks away. It was too loud to talk, and I think that we were both relieved. The music was awful, but we stayed through the final set anyway, then flagged a taxi. In the backseat, Leda lay her head on my shoulder and fell asleep as soon as the car started moving.

Blue Door:
A Collection
of Passings

Morning: she brings him an orange. Knocking on the blue door of his flat. He thuds down stairs, opens the door to street sunlight. A lily in her hair, she outstretches her arms: an orange in her hands. Behind her a boy bicycles—tossing rolled up news onto doorsteps. Women walk down the street for apricots, zucchini, jars of honey, jam. Someone is frying eggs—the street smells like breakfast. He leans against the blue door; she holds the orange to him in both hands. Behind her an old man smokes a cigar, waving and laughing to babies strolling past. A blue-suited man walks hurriedly with a cardboard tube under his arm. An old woman bends, watering gardenias in front of the flats across the street. Leaning against the blue-painted door: his hand through his ginger hair; she cups her hands with orange. A woman round with baby chases after a giggling boy; the father carries a brown paper bag in each arm. Bicycles with baskets lean against black lampposts. Little girls jump rope. A woman sits on her steps, holding a blue mug to her lips. He looks at the doorstep; she looks at him: orange in her hands. A man walks past with a carton of red strawberries—holding green stem, biting sweet ruby. Two brothers play jacks on the sidewalk. Drumming his fingers on blue wood, he breathes into his chest; she smells sweetly of orange. Up the street, women carry brown bags of apricots, zucchini, jars of honey, jam. The sun is high. An old man smoking a cigar puts his finger to his lips, smiling at mothers pushing strollers. Across the street, kids jump down steps, lift bicycles from lampposts, ride down the street yelling front and back to each other. A woman calls the boys in from playing jacks. A blue-suited man slowly passes. Someone is grilling salmon—the street smells of fire and charcoal. The sun melts pink. Kids lean bicycles against lighted lampposts. Slowly she lowers her hands, dropping the orange into her straw bag; he closes the door blue. Stubbing out his cigar, the old man looks up at the rising moon: white, round, quiet as regret above Evening Street. Walking past lit windows he stops at a door, turns a long key, pulls a lamp string to walls lit with paintings: hung, taped, leaning from tables. Paintings large as doorways, small as postcards. Paintings drying on newspaper, standing on easels. Paintings: swirls of colored oil—where her hands cup an orange.

Adrift

The rainstorm came on all at once—a pelting, August rain that no one, it seemed, had anticipated, as there wasn't a single umbrella open anywhere on the street. Sina grabbed Lewis's arm and they ran toward the red awning at the entrance of the three-story brick building. Across the street to their right, Lake Ontario was a deep blue-gray and beginning to swell with waves.

"Should we get a table?" Sina asked as Lewis opened the door.

"We should at least get on the list."

They stepped inside the high-ceilinged space with its exposed pipes, brick walls, and tiled floor.

"Two?" the young woman asked from behind the host stand.

Her hair was pulled back into a tight bun, which stretched the corners of her eyes.

"Three," Sina said. "We're meeting someone."

"Name?"

"Lewis." Sina always gave Lewis's name instead of her own.

The woman wrote down the name. "The wait right now is thirty minutes."

Sina and Lewis walked over to the bar and took the two tall chairs left. When the bartender looked up at them, Sina ordered a glass of white wine, and Lewis asked for the local beer on tap.

"How long has it been since you've seen him?" Sina asked, slipping her arms into the white sweater she had draped over her shoulders. Her dark bangs were matted to her forehead from the rain.

"Five years."

The bartender set their drinks on the bar, and as they sipped them they occasionally glanced behind themselves at the door.

"I'm nervous to meet him," Sina said.

"How come?"

"He is kind of famous, you know."

Outside the rain was growing heavier. They listened to it pound down on the roof. It was almost seven, the time they were supposed to meet Christo.

"I wish I would have read one of his books," Sina said, sipping her wine. It was already half gone. "They're crime novels?"

"Mysteries." Lewis looked into the mirror beneath the liquor bottles and brushed his thinning hair forward with his fingers. "Literary mysteries, I guess. If there is such a thing."

"Are they good?"

"Yeah. The ones I've read."

They were quiet for a while, and without meaning to, Sina took the last sip of her wine. When the bartender asked if she wanted another glass she looked once more at the door before saying yes.

"Be careful of having too much too soon," Lewis said. "You need to learn how to pace yourself."

"It was a skimpy glass. I'll sip this one slowly."

At twenty past seven, Sina asked Lewis if they were at the right restaurant.

He nodded.

At seven thirty, she asked if he thought that something might have happened.

"No. He was always late for class too."

The restaurant was growing more crowded by the minute. The line at the host stand was now snaking out the door and beneath the awning. Each time the door opened and closed the smell from the fish shanty across the street wafted into the restaurant.

"Did he say anything about his wife?" Sina asked carefully, trying not to pry.

"No. I don't know anything more than what Sam told me on the phone."

"How long has she been missing now?"

"Three months."

"And they still haven't found the boat?"

"No."

Sina sipped her wine. "I find it strange that she took the boat out alone. Without telling anyone."

Lewis shrugged. "She grew up on a sailboat in Albania."

"I thought she was American."

"She was born in the states but went to Durrës to live with her grandparents when she was young. They sent her back when she was a teenager because of some relationship she got involved in. I forget the details." Lewis lifted his empty glass and made eye contact with the bartender.

"Christo told you this?"

"She did."

Sina swiveled her chair to face Lewis. "You've met her?"

"I lived here for two years. Of course I met her. A bunch of times."

The bartender took Lewis's empty glass and set a full pint in its place.

"What was she like?"

"Intelligent. Frank, but not rude."

"What did she look like?"

"She had reddish hair. It was always a little messy. She was lean, kind of athletic-looking. I don't think I ever saw her in shoes."

"Not even in winter?"

"You're really asking a lot of questions tonight," Lewis said.

"Sorry. I've just never had dinner with a man whose wife is missing. I'm worried I'll say something stupid."

"Don't ask about her, and you'll be fine." Lewis sipped his beer. Then looking behind him, he said, "He's here."

Sina turned around and saw a man in a wrinkled linen shirt, a lightweight checked sports coat, khaki pants, and boat shoes, one of them untied. His whitish-blonde hair was damp, his face unshaven. He was using a long umbrella as a cane, and he looked around the restaurant before spotting Lewis at the bar.

Lewis met him halfway to the door, and Sina slid off her chair. She watched Lewis and Christo shake hands and give each other the sort of half hug that men give to other men. Then the two of them walked over to the bar.

"Christo, this is my fiancée, Sina."

Sina reached her hand to Christo, and he squeezed it in his warm grip.

"We put our name on the list for a table," Lewis said. "It shouldn't be much longer."

Christo looked at Lewis's half-full beer and asked the bartender for a Scotch. Then he slid a ten-dollar bill across the bar and stood next to Sina.

"Do you want to sit down?" Sina asked.

"No," he said. "I prefer to stand. It's easier on my back."

The bartender set Christo's Scotch on the bar as the hostess approached, holding three menus. "I can show you to your table now."

The three of them sat down at a table in the middle of the restaurant—Sina and Lewis across from each other and Christo in between. The woman handed them each a menu, which they set on the table unopened. Right away a waiter appeared. He was young, in his early twenties. The cuffs of his white shirt were stained with sauce. "Good evening. My name is Jesse. I'm lucky enough to be your server tonight. Can I bring you anything else to drink?"

"I'll have another glass of Sauvignon Blanc," Sina said. "The one from New Zealand."

Lewis glared at her from across the table, but Sina looked away. "Anybody else?"

Lewis and Christo shook their heads.

"What's it been—two, three years since I've seen you?" Christo asked Lewis.

"I was just telling Sina that I haven't been up here in five years. Since the spring I took the job in Baltimore."

Christo sipped his drink. "I lose track of the years." He turned to Sina. "I'm only sixty-three, even though I look like I'm a hundred."

"You do not," Sina said.

"Well, I walk like I'm eighty. You can't argue with that. Though I still have my sea legs."

The waiter appeared and set Sina's wine glass in front of her. "Have you had a chance to look at the menu?"

"Not yet," Christo said. "We'll take some time."

"Certainly, sir. There's no rush. Enjoy your drinks." The waiter bowed before leaving the table.

"The waiters are too damn friendly in this town," Christo said.

"It's a nice change for us," Sina said. "We just spent two weeks in Europe being ignored by waiters."

"What were you doing over there?"

"Visiting friends. Though Lewis spent most of his time writing."

Christo looked at Lewis. "Did you ever finish that novel?"

"It died on me. But I've recently gone back to the first story I workshopped in your class. I'm turning it into a novella, and it's going pretty well."

"Which story?"

"The one with the candy store scene."

"I couldn't admit this to you at the time," Christo said, reaching again for his Scotch, "but I was jealous when I read that."

"What candy store scene?" Sina asked.

Lewis sipped his beer. "Basically a guy runs into an ex-girlfriend at a candy store when he's traveling in Peru."

"Doesn't he leave his wife at the end of that story?" Christo asked.

"He doesn't actually leave her, but the reader is led to believe that he will."

"Send me a draft when it's finished. I'll be curious to read it."

"It's going to be a while," Lewis said. "The paper takes just about all my time."

"It's true," Sina said. "I almost feel like I live alone. We have dinner together once or twice a week."

The waiter returned to the table. "Have you decided?"

"I suppose we'd better take a look at these things," Christo said, opening his menu. He took out a pair of reading glasses from the inside pocket of his coat, and the waiter left the table. "The walleye here is of course excellent. It's caught right out there." He gestured toward the lake. "You can get it broiled or fried. Both are good. I've had a couple of the pasta dishes. They're also known for their steaks. Aside from the waiters, you can't go wrong here."

When the waiter returned, Sina ordered the broiled walleye, and Lewis and Christo ordered it fried.

"And bring us a bottle of whatever she's drinking," Christo said. "Two more glasses."

"Certainly, sir," the waiter said, coming out with the bottle a few minutes later. He opened it at the table and poured a little for Christo to taste.

"Fine," Christo said, and the waiter filled his glass halfway, then poured a glass for Lewis.

"This is good," Christo said, tilting his glass toward Sina.

She smiled.

"Bring another bottle of this with our meals," he said to the waiter, who gave a slight bow before walking away. Then Christo turned to Sina and Lewis. "Well, I suppose you heard what happened." He took another sip of wine. "I was at the grocery store. Grocery shopping has always been my responsibility. Klea does most of the cooking." He crossed his legs, and his napkin fell to the floor. He reached down to pick it up. "When I got home and saw that the boat was gone, I didn't think anything of it. When she didn't return by dinnertime, I took the motor boat out and had a look around our usual sailing spots. Then I motored home and called the police. By nine o'clock we had a search party going." Christo finished the wine in his glass and poured himself half a glass more.

"Did you find anything at all?" Sina asked.

Lewis shot her a look.

"The coast guard found a life preserver in the seaway the next morning, but it wasn't one of ours."

"If there's anything I can do—" Lewis said.

"It's all been done," said Christo. "Having dinner with an old friend is a welcome change in my routine."

Lewis poured himself more wine, then looked at Sina's nearly empty glass and reluctantly poured her another inch. Sina looked directly at him, reached for the bottle, and poured herself two inches more.

"I had a dog go missing when I was growing up," she said. "The waiting and wondering were excruciating."

"Of course she doesn't mean to compare your wife's disappearance to that of a dog's," Lewis said, staring at Sina.

"A dog is an important part of any family," Christo said.

The waiter returned with the second bottle of wine, though the first was not yet empty, and they sipped their wine while making small talk—Christo asking Lewis about the *Baltimore Sun*, Lewis asking Christo about his novel coming out in the fall. When Christo began filling Lewis in on people he'd known in the past—the university president who had divorced and remarried twice in the last four years; a physics professor who had left his position to open a bakery, which he closed three months later to revive a tree farm in Québec—Sina slipped away from the table. On her way to the restroom she walked through the dining room among tables high and low, passing the host stand near the door, still crowded with people though the line no longer stretched outside. When she reached the bar she considered ordering a drink and pretending, for a few moments, to be someone else, but the thought drifted away so quickly that she'd barely had the chance to notice it.

The meals had arrived while she was gone, and when she sat down at the table she took a bite of her fish. "This is delicious," she said to Christo.

"One of the many pleasures of living here."

"I miss it," Lewis said. "The fish and the town."

Christo wiped the tartar sauce from his lips with his napkin. "Have you two set a date?"

"We're thinking September of next year," Sina said at the same time that Lewis said "No."

Sina and Lewis looked at each other.

"I guess we're still working it out," Sina said, embarrassed.

"How is everything tasting?" the waiter asked, appearing across from Christo.

"Fine, fine," Christo said, waving him away with his wine glass. "We'll call you over when we need you."

The three of them ate their meals without saying much more, the din of the conversations around them eliminating the pressure to speak. When they had finished, the waiter came to clear their dishes. "Dessert for anyone? Coffee?"

"Not for me," Christo said. "Perhaps for these two."

"I'd split something with you," Sina said, looking across the table at Lewis.

But Lewis shook his head. "I'm full."

The waiter came back a few minutes later with the bill, which Christo paid, ignoring Lewis's attempts to pay the bill himself.

The rain had turned to drizzle by the time they stepped outside.

"Where are you staying?" Christo asked.

"The Beacon," said Lewis.

"Next time you'll stay with me."

"We'd love that," Sina said.

Sina and Lewis watched Christo walk beneath his umbrella, the blue and white checks of his jacket blending into a solid pewter as he moved farther away, the brick buildings of town looking almost red beneath the misty gray sky.

"Well?" Lewis said. "The hotel?"

Sina held her sweater above her head to block the light rain as they walked up the hill, away from the lake.

The hotel lobby was crowded with women in dresses and men in suits, and there was music—a live jazz band—coming from the ballroom. A bride was sitting on one of the sofas, drinking a glass of wine and talking with one of her purple-gowned bridesmaids.

Sina and Lewis maneuvered through the crowd, passing the front desk on their way to the elevator, which they rode up to the fourth floor. Down the hall, Lewis unlocked the door to room 417 and stepped inside behind Sina. The bed had been made, and fresh towels were hanging in the bathroom. The heavy brown drapes had been pulled open, but the translucent curtains behind them remained drawn. Only a sliver of window shown in between.

"Do you think there's any chance they'll find Christo's wife?" Sina asked, hanging her sweater on the back of the armchair to dry.

"No."

"What makes you say no?"

"Three months is a long time to be gone." Lewis sat down on the bed. He grabbed his book from the nightstand and lay back against the pillows.

"Do you think she drowned?"

"Most likely."

Sina changed into her nightshirt, then went into the bathroom where she used the toilet, washed her face, and brushed her teeth. "I'm exhausted," she said, flopping onto the bed beside Lewis.

"I think I'm going to go downstairs for a nightcap."

"Why are you saying that now—after I changed and got ready for bed?"

"You just said that you're exhausted."

"I could have had one drink with you. A hot tea even."

"I just thought of it. I'm not tired, and you're going to sleep." Lewis got up. "It's only nine thirty," he said, then left the room.

Sina lay in bed, listening to the rattling of the air conditioner. After a while she turned off the lamp, then immediately turned it back on. She didn't feel tired anymore. Never remembering to pack a book for herself, she reached for Lewis's book on the nightstand and began to read, but her mind kept drifting back to Christo's wife alone on the sailboat, her auburn hair blowing in the wind.

She considered getting dressed and going downstairs, but she didn't want Lewis to accuse her of checking up on him. Instead she made a cup of tea with the mint tea bag next to the coffee maker on the dresser, and she sat in bed, drinking it as slowly as she could. The water was not very hot to begin with, however, so it wasn't too long before she set the empty cup on the dresser and reached for the remote. Turning on the TV, she began flipping through the local news programs and previews for the movies that she could rent, but she quickly grew bored and turned the TV off along with the lamp. Then she lay there waiting in the darkened room, the streetlamps shining through the window and illuminating the sheer curtains like two sails glowing in moonlight.

Rescue

They were having breakfast in their small apartment on the outskirts of the city. It was a Sunday morning in August, quiet save for the clatter of the train on the raised tracks behind their building. Each time the train rumbled by, shaking their coffee cups and rattling their spoons, Lulu, their four-month-old puppy, would dash to the window and bark—the hair on her back raised. "Lulu," the man called to her after the third train had passed. "Come." She barked deeply once more, then squeezed under the table between their legs, whimpering. The man reached his hand to pat her on the head. "She'll get used to it," he said, spreading orange marmalade onto a piece of toast with the spoon sticking out of the jar. He took a bite of the crunchy bread moistened by the gooey fruit, then sipped his coffee. Underneath the table, the woman rubbed Lulu's back with her foot, imagining that she could feel the striped colors of her coat—yellow, dark gray, bits of white and orangish brown. They'd found Lulu at five weeks, half-starved and asleep behind the dumpster. She'd looked like a malnourished tiger cub, born months too soon. They'd immediately taken her to a vet, who instructed them to rub honey on her lips and to mix Pedialyte with her water until she started eating. After three days, Lulu took her first bite of food. It had been late at night, and the man and woman were in bed when they heard the unmistakable sound of her teeth crunching the dry kibble. Now, at the breakfast table, it was the woman who wasn't eating. She was looking out the window at the loose railing of the balcony and at the grill that must have been emitting a host of alluring smells. "What's wrong?" the man asked. The woman lifted her eyes to his. "Nothing. I'm just having a hard time waking up." "Didn't you sleep well?" "I slept deeply," she said, "but I had another dream about Lu." The man set down his coffee cup. "What was this one about?" he asked. "The three of us were at a beach on the ocean. You were swimming very far out, and Lulu and I were sitting on a blanket in the sand. We were watching you rise and fall in the rolling waves, swimming farther and farther out. Lu wasn't on a leash, and I was holding her ribs between my hands while keeping my eyes on you as you floated in the clear, deep water. Then Lulu broke loose and started running toward the sea, kicking up sand as I darted after her, reaching for an ear—her collar—a hind leg—her tail—anything that would help me get ahold of her, but I couldn't catch her. And just before she reached the water she turned into a turtle—a sea turtle with a hard shell and webbed feet. She scurried to the water's edge and began swimming—gliding through the water quickly and effortlessly. I fell in after her, diving down again and again—my eyes burning from the salt as I looked for her everywhere, reaching my arms all around. You started looking for her, too—both of us afraid that she would swim away, get lost, not know how to feed herself or how to keep safe. We were stretching our arms as wide as they would go—so wide we felt that our bodies might split in half. Then suddenly I saw her in front of me—her turtle head bobbing and her feet flapping as she swam by. I grabbed her—clutching her rounded shell between my palms. I turned toward shore and kicked my legs as hard as I could. I kicked and kicked and grew exhausted, unable to use my arms to help. Once my feet touched the sand, I ran—holding Lu out of the water in front of me, her scaled legs moving as if she were swimming, like she did when you first held her above the bathtub. I was grasping her so tightly that I felt her slippery underside compress, and I was worried that she couldn't breathe, but I kept squeezing her and running—running away from the ocean." The man reached his foot to touch the dog under the table, as if to make sure she was still there. He felt her hairless stomach, smooth against his toes, and he listened as she softly licked her paws. Then, taking a sip of coffee, he began to rub her neck, moving his foot back and forth rhythmically, soothingly—relieved that she'd once again survived.

Before
the Story
Ends

PROLOGUE

Once upon a time, in a very large city, your father owned a letterpress printshop, and your mother sold hats. Each weekday, at five in the afternoon, your father would close up the printshop, locking the door at the same time your mother locked the hat shop one district over. They would take different trains to their small flats—his on the third floor, hers on the fourth. Your mother would pour a glass of wine and your father a beer. They would stand at their windows, looking out at the people below on the sidewalks stepping into restaurants or out of the shops in the sunny or dark or snowy or rainy afternoon just before it transformed into evening, then night.

One afternoon, when business was slow, your mother opened the phone book and looked under *L*. She closed her eyes and slid her pointer finger down the long list of printshops that, due to the recent revival of the letterpress, had popped up all over the city. She stopped her finger, opened her eyes, and dialed the number.

"Printshop," your father said into the phone.

"Hello," said your mother. "I'm looking to have a sign made— for my hat shop. Do you make signs?"

"I can."

"And what do you charge?"

"It depends on the number of words, of course, on the paper you choose, and on whether you want colored ink or just black. The typeface must also be taken into consideration. Is it possible for you to stop by?"

"I suppose I could," your mother said, and your mother and father hung up their phones.

The next morning, your mother took an early lunch, leaving the shop at a little past eleven. She took the subway two stops. Then, carrying a striped hat box in one arm, she walked beneath her umbrella in the cool autumn drizzle, looking into the windows of a stationery shop, an art gallery, and two empty storefronts before she came upon the correct address.

Your father was typesetting a menu for the restaurant opening next door when the bell jingled and your mother stepped inside. Dropping her umbrella into the wooden stand by the door, she breathed in the metallic scent of ink and unbuttoned her raincoat. Then she looked around the cramped studio, smoothing her auburn hair. At the sight of her, your father, a man of average height with broad shoulders and a noticeable sense of quietude, stood up straight and rolled down his sleeves.

"Hello," your mother said. "I called yesterday—about the sign?"

"For your hat shop," your father said. "Please." He gestured toward the composing table that stood in front of the press.

Your mother and father sat down on two metal stools.

"I'm _____," he said, reaching his hand toward your mother.

"Pleased to meet you," she said. "My name is _____."

(Your mother asked that their names be left out, for if you are not named, she wished, in this story, that they not be named either.)

"So," your father said. "You need a sign for your business?"

"Yes. I mean, in part." Your mother looked at her hands, and your father leaned forward, resting his elbows on the table. He sensed your mother's hesitance, and he waited patiently for her to continue. "It's probably a stupid idea," she said.

"Let's hear it before you rule it out."

"All right." Your mother straightened her posture. "I was thinking about a sign that brings men into the shop. To help me find the man whose head perfectly fits this hat." Out of the box on her lap she took a dark brown trilby and set it on the table.

Your father looked closely at the hat and saw that it was cut from a very fine wool, and only when he turned it in his hands did the faint blue lines of a plaid pattern emerge.

"It's very handsome," he said, running his finger along the short, slightly downturned brim in the front and around to the back where it flipped up. Where do you get your hats?"

"I make them," your mother said.

"You made this hat?"

She nodded. "I studied with Santiago del Soto. You may have heard of him—he's quite well known in the industry."

"I can't say that I have." Your father was still studying the hat. "Can I ask you, though, what gave you the idea for this—quest?"

"Cinderella, I guess." Your mother looked out the window at a woman in sweats pushing a jogging stroller. "It's dumb, I know."

"I think it's brilliant," your father said. "Men love games. They'll be trampling over each other to get into your shop, and once they're inside they'll be overcome with desire for one of your beautiful hats." He was genuinely excited about the idea. "What happens when you find a winner?"

"Like I said," your mother replied. "Cinderella." Her eyes briefly met your father's. "You'd be surprised by the particular shape of a man's head."

"Oh," your father said, suddenly understanding. "But what if the hat fits . . . what if the hat fits someone whom you'd rather it not?"

"I guess I'll take my chances," your mother said.

"Well," said your father, "we should start with the wording. Have you given it any thought?"

"Not really."

He got up for a notebook and a pencil, then sat back down. "It might be helpful if you describe for me the hat-fitting process."

"First a man would come into the shop," your mother began, "after reading the sign, of course, and I would ask him to sit in a chair while I take the hat from its box. Then I would set the hat on his head and pull it down very gently, feeling for a good fit. It's important that I put the hat on him so that he doesn't stretch the fabric, trying to force it." She looked at the wooden shelf stacked with cans of ink. "I guess that's assuming that a man would try such a thing."

"Of course he would—any man would." Your father felt his cheeks grow hot, and he quickly looked down at his notebook, arbitrarily writing and underlining the words hat-fitting process. "What happens next?" he asked.

"I suppose that depends on whether or not the hat fits."

"Right," your father said. It was clear that he didn't know where to begin.

"Maybe it would help to run through the process right now," your mother said, reaching the hat toward him. She set the hat on his head, then pulled at it very gently until it sat just above his ears. It fit perfectly. She slowly took her hands away, and your mother and father looked into each other's eyes. When most people would have looked away, they did not. Your mother reached her hands to your father's head, taking the hat off and putting it back on. It still fit. Exactly.

The clock tower outside began chiming. It was two districts away, but they could hear it as if it were right outside the window. "I no longer want to make this sign," your father said, very quietly and very seriously. And before your mother could reply, he reached his calloused hand to her cheek and leaned in to kiss her.

It was a gentle kiss. Effortless and sure of itself. Not one of those kisses that stutters or fumbles for its way. It was a kiss that knew what it was doing, and because of this, it lasted the perfect amount of time, both sets of lips withdrawing at the exact same moment.

The next day, at the courthouse, your mother and father were married. They couldn't afford a honeymoon, so they spent the week unpacking boxes in their new flat—slightly larger than both of their previous flats put together, and in a more desirable neighborhood. There was a claw-foot tub in the bathroom and a black-and-white-tiled floor in the kitchen. They painted the living room walls a very soft gray, which looked beautiful with the white crown molding, the white built-in bookshelves, and the white French doors that opened to the iron balcony, overlooking the crowded storefronts below. When the flat was nearly ready, the wooden floor gleamed in the sunlight as your mother hung their drawings and your father, wearing his hat, opened a bottle of champagne.

They returned to work the following week, meeting at noon each day at a small café on the edge of the park to eat the sandwiches your mother had packed. But one day, in mid-December, the mere thought of the tuna fish sandwiches your mother had made that morning had prompted her to call your father just in time to cancel their lunch. After hanging up the phone she locked the front door of the shop and changed the sign in the window from open to closed. She walked quickly to the tiny bathroom in the back and, kneeling on the floor in front of the toilet, became sick.

With each heave came the urge to heave again. For what seemed like hours, she was violently ill. Then all of a sudden she felt well. She stood up and rinsed her mouth at the sink. She wiped the black smudges from beneath her eyes and put on her coat. She walked across the street to the pharmacy, came out with a small brown bag, then unlocked the door of the hat shop and relocked it behind her.

In the bathroom she opened the box and unfolded the piece of paper. She read the directions, sat down on the seat, and took the test. The small white circle stared at her as she waited. She waited forever. Then, gradually, as if by magic, the faint outline of a gold star began to appear—five sparkling points meeting in the center. Holding the wand in one hand, she reread the directions. She reread them three more times before she was sure that she was not mistaken. Then she looked again at the star. She was pregnant with you.

5

"I'm going to be late coming home," your mother said into the telephone to your father. "I'll pick something up for dinner, so we don't have to cook."

"Is everything all right?" your father asked.

"I just have a few things to do before I lock up."

"Are you sure there's nothing wrong?"

"I just need to double check a few things before I end the day. I'll feel much better if I do."

Your father was pleased enough with this answer, so they hung up their phones.

The sky was growing dark and very clear when your mother left the hat shop. She pushed her hands into the pockets of her coat as she walked briskly down the street. Eight blocks later when she reached the glass building, she took the elevator up to the seventh floor and walked down the hall to Suite B. She stood at the check-in counter and gave the receptionist her name. The receptionist found her name on the schedule and told her to have a seat. The nurse would be with her shortly.

Your mother sat down on one of the blue-cushioned seats in the waiting area. There were other women waiting as well, many of them with round stomachs that your mother tried not to notice. She looked at a magazine, at the muted television, at the ticking clock on the wall.

"_____?" the nurse called, and your mother stood up, dropping the magazine onto the coffee table in front of her. She followed the nurse down the hall to the scale, then behind a curtain where the nurse sat down in front of a computer and your mother on a chair beside her.

"Your reason for coming in?" the nurse asked.

"I think I may be pregnant."

"Did you take a test?"

"Yes."

"And you saw a—"

"Star," your mother said.

"The first day of your last period?"

"October nineteenth."

"You're fairly certain about that?"

"Positive."

The nurse counted weeks on the round calendar wheel that she took from her white coat pocket. "That puts you at seven weeks and four days. Your due date will be July twenty-seventh." She wrote something down in her folder. "Any morning sickness?"

"As of today."

"Other symptoms?"

"My breasts are sore."

"They should become less tender when you reach your second trimester—at around twelve or thirteen weeks."

After leading your mother down the hall to a small room with a cot, a stool, and two wooden chairs, the nurse opened a cupboard and took out a thin sheet folded neatly into a square. "Everything off from your waist down. You can cover up with this. The doctor will be in soon."

Twenty minutes after the nurse had left the room, there was a brief knock at the door. Then the doctor, a tall woman wearing a white coat, entered, pushing a machine on wheels. "This is going to feel a little cold," she said, squirting a gooey substance from a plastic bottle with a blue tip onto your mother's bare lower abdomen. Then she took the probe and began pressing it in circles below your mother's bellybutton while your mother and the doctor looked at the screen attached to the machine. "This is the inside of your uterus," the doctor said.

On the screen was a triangular black and white image. It looked as if it were moving, but it was only the probe that moved. Your mother's uterus was still.

"Sometimes they're hard to find when they're so tiny," the doctor said. She kept moving the probe and watching for you to appear on the screen.

"Is there any chance that I could be wrong?" your mother asked. She was starting to worry.

"Not if you had a positive pregnancy test," the doctor said. "Of course there's always the chance that you could have miscarried. Have you noticed any bleeding?"

"No. None."

The doctor lifted the probe from your mother's stomach and

wiped the gel off with a towel. "We'll have to go the other route. Scoot down and slide your feet into the stirrups."

Your mother did as she was asked.

The doctor used a different probe to look for you from another perspective. The same image appeared on the screen: a black and white triangular shape that seemed to move as the doctor moved the probe. When you still didn't appear, your mother began to feel as if she'd lost you, even though she was never sure that you had been there in the first place.

"The tilt of your uterus is the problem," the doctor said. "This machine doesn't have a high enough frequency to see at such an angle." She took one more look around for you before removing the probe. Then the doctor took off her gloves, washed her hands, and walked out, leaving your mother alone in the room, not knowing if you existed, and if you did, where you were.

The nurse peeked her head into the room. "You'll need to get dressed," she said.

Your mother put on her clothes.

A few minutes later the nurse returned, and your mother followed her down the long hallway with soft green walls and a green tile floor, turning left, then right, then left again. They stopped at an open door, next to which stood a woman, middle-aged and mild. Her hair was red and her smile was cautious. "I'm Sarah," she said. "I'll be doing your exam."

Your mother followed Sarah into the room, much darker than the room she'd just left. There were no overhead lights, only the dim glow of a few upturned lamps attached to the walls. Sarah handed your mother a sheet, then stepped out of the room while she undressed. When she was lying on the cot, her feet in the stirrups, Sarah knocked on the door and entered. She sat down on a swiveling stool beside the cot, turning the screen away from your mother and toward herself. She inserted the probe and watched the screen while your mother held her breath and looked at the ceiling. Then Sarah turned the screen and your mother saw you for the first time: a tiny white figure moving around inside a dark circle.

"That flashing light is what we're looking for," Sarah said. "That's the heartbeat."

Your mother watched your heart beat on the screen, like a faraway star flashing in the night sky.

"This is the head, and these look to me like two little arm buds." Sarah drew lines on the screen with the mouse, measuring you and taking photographs.

Your mother reached her finger toward you. She might have been imagining it, but she saw you move, just a little, when she touched the screen.

"So everything's—fine?" your mother asked.

"The baby looks perfectly healthy," Sarah said. Then she took out the probe and you disappeared. After typing something into the computer she printed two photographs of you, one above the other on the same narrow sheet of paper. She handed the photographs to your mother, smiled at her, then left the room.

Your mother sat on the cot, looking at you closely in the dim light. In the first picture, the one on top, you were facing upward—as if looking at the sky. In the lower picture, you were facing your mother. She could see your eyelids, and below them the mark of a nose and the tiny curve that had to be your lips. You were hugging yourself with your little arm buds and the two white dots of your feet. It would be thirteen weeks before the ultrasound would be able to tell your sex, but your mother already knew that you were a girl.

4

Your mother opened the door of the apartment building and stepped inside the drafty foyer. She stood in the light of the chandelier, searching her purse until she found you between the pages of a hardcover book. Then she carried you up to the second floor.

Your father was setting the table with the good china when your mother entered the apartment. He turned around, a dinner plate in his hand.

"They almost couldn't find her," your mother said, barely getting the words out. She handed the photographs of you to your father. "It took them three tries, then all of a sudden she was there. I saw her little heart blinking on the screen."

Your father looked at you very closely. Then he lifted his eyes toward your mother. "We're having a—"

Your mother nodded.

Your father stared at you some more. "She looks like you," he said. "I can't believe how much she looks like you."

Your mother moved close to him, and they looked at you together, the moonlight shining through the windows and drowning out the lamps. "But she has your personality," your mother said. "She's so calm."

Your mother's stomach began to growl, and your father said, "Looks like the little one wants her dinner."

"Dinner," your mother said. "I didn't bring anything home."

Your father smiled and touched your mother low on her belly. He kissed her on the forehead, and without discussing it, they headed down the stairs and across the street to Bistro Armand.

At a table for two by the window your father ordered a glass of wine and your mother a mineral water. The waiter brought them a basket of bread, which you and your mother had finished before he'd had a chance to take out his pen.

"Looks like we'll need more bread," your father said happily to the waiter, and your mother blushed.

When the waiter left the table, your mother leaned back in her chair. "Now we know she has expensive taste," she said with a laugh.

"That was my fear," said your father. And he laughed too, reaching for his wine.

That night the three of you had your first dinner as a family, at the little bistro with the rose-colored walls. Of course you had been together for weeks before your parents knew you were there. You had already been growing rapidly, your cells dividing and multiplying and taking on specific functions. Your brain, spinal cord, and heart, for example, had begun to develop two weeks prior, when you'd first become an embryo, and two weeks before that, as a zygote, you'd spent eight days traveling down your mother's Fallopian tube on your way toward becoming a morula, then a blastocyst. When you were nine days old, exhausted, you reached her womb, and on day ten, your mother had to have known on some very deep level that you had implanted yourself into her uterine wall.

In bed that night, your mother had a dream. She was walking up the concrete stairs of a very tall building. There was no elevator. Only a never-ending staircase. Then suddenly a woman appeared from one of the emergency exit doors. She was wearing a white lab coat and holding a clipboard. She called your mother's name.

"_____?" the woman said.

Your mother turned her head.

"Come with me," said the woman.

Your mother followed her through the door and down a long greenish hallway lit with bright fluorescent lights. The woman walked quickly, and your mother could barely keep up. With each step your mother took, the woman was two steps farther ahead. They passed a number of closed metal doors. The doors looked to your mother as if they would be very cold if she touched them. Through one of the doors, she could hear the sound of infants crying. Your mother slowed down, turning her head toward the sound. She stopped walking, spun around, and headed back for that door.

The woman realized that your mother was not following her, and she too turned around, marching toward your mother. Just as your mother was about to touch the doorknob, the woman took her by the elbow. "This way," she said sternly, and she led your mother down the hallway, away from the closed door, the crying beginning to fade.

Then your mother woke up, the ticking of the clock on her nightstand matching the rhythm of the footsteps in her dream. She put her hand on her abdomen and moved it around. She slid out of bed and tiptoed to the bathroom. The tile floor was cold against her bare feet, and the porcelain seat even colder when she sat down. Lifting her nightshirt, she looked down at her flat stomach and willed it to grow. She needed some proof that you were still there.

3

When your father got out of bed at six o'clock, as he did every morning, your mother was sitting at the dining room table still set with china from the night before, a cup of lemon tea cooling before her.

"If I don't look at the pictures," your mother said, watching for the first hint of light to appear above the apartment building across the street, "I have a hard time believing that she's real."

"She's real," your father said. "Give her some time to become real in your mind."

Later that morning, at the printshop, the sun shone through the windows as your father opened a large, flat drawer of the short paper cabinet and took out a stack of 7 × 7 Magnani Arturo, stationery cards imported from Italy that he used only for the highest paying clients. He set the deckle-edged cards on the table, grabbed a composing stick, and turning toward the tall cabinet, opened to the case of French italic type. He began working on the last set of New Year's Eve party invitations, a task so large that, for the past two months, it had shortened his weekends and lengthened his weeks.

That afternoon, your mother waited on the underground platform for the train that would take her to the school of design where she had studied for three years before opening her hat shop. She had read in the paper that Santiago was giving a lecture on the effect of chance on aesthetics, and she had closed the shop early in order to attend.

When she got off the train in the fashion district, she rode the steep escalator up to ground level and walked toward the cluster of brick buildings that comprised the school. She entered the building to the left of the fountain and headed toward the main lecture hall, just off the lobby. When she saw the sign on the closed door that read "del Soto lecture cancelled," she asked a young man standing in front of the side entrance to the building, a backpack slung over his shoulder, if he'd heard anything about it.

"Rumor is that Santiago has nothing more to say about hats," he said, and he pushed open the glass door.

Your mother followed him out of the building and continued down the street, passing the apartment building where her friend, Isla, had lived during their studies, the convenience store where they'd often bought cheap Hungarian wine to drink in her kitchen at the end of the week, and the row of student-run boutiques that came and went every few months—some occasionally sticking around for a year. She didn't recognize any of the boutiques save for the one on the corner with blue and gold paper stars hanging in the window.

A bell jingled when your mother stepped inside. There were three racks of clothes—one pushed against each side wall and one standing freely in the middle. In the back were two dressing rooms hung with heavy curtains, and between them a trifold mirror in front of which sat a worn, carpeted platform. This boutique—a shop for expecting mothers—had been around even before your mother had first come to this neighborhood to apply to the school. It had been opened by one of the students just after he'd graduated, and no one had thought that it would survive. This was a neighborhood for students and young couples just starting out, not a place for families. But the maternity boutique was still in business.

Your mother flipped through the racks until, draped over her arm, she had all the dresses that she could carry. Behind one of the curtains she tried on a Persian-blue dress that reached her knees, a deep purple dress that tied behind her neck, a long black dress covered in sequins, a short silver dress with long sleeves, and three or four others. Only the last one she tried on, a shiny green dress with an empire waist and very thin straps, prompted her to slide open the curtain and stand in front of the trifold mirror. Turning this way and that, she looked at herself from every angle, pulling on the extra fabric around her waist.

"You're not going to need all that room," a woman said.

Your mother turned around.

The woman looked to be younger than your mother by a few years—in her late twenties. Her blond hair was pulled back in a ponytail, and her swollen belly protruded beneath her long gray sweater, which she wore over a pair of black leggings and underneath an unbuttoned coat. She was sifting through the middle rack, gathering a pile of blouses.

"You think I need a smaller size?" your mother asked her.

"No," the woman said, briefly looking up at your mother. "It fits you in the bust, and the straps lay nicely."

Your mother continued to look at her. "I don't understand, then."

"The dress looks very pretty on you. I just don't think you're going to need all that room in the middle."

The girl behind the counter, most likely a student, was leaning on her elbows and looking at your mother. She was clearly listening to the conversation, but she remained silent.

Your mother stepped behind the curtain. She took her sweater from the foldout chair, rolled it into a ball, then slid it beneath the dress and up to her belly. Turning from side to side, she looked at herself in the mirror. With a rounder stomach, she thought the dress would fit her perfectly. But she didn't feel that she could buy the dress when the woman seemed to be advising her not to, and when the salesgirl didn't object.

Reluctantly leaving the shop, your mother walked toward the bakery—another neighborhood business she'd been surprised as a student to discover. It was one of the great finds in the city, and, as is the case with most great finds, they're not where you expect them to be.

It was nearly four o'clock, and the daylight was beginning to fade when your mother opened the glass door and took her place in line at the counter. Looking at the cupcakes, date bars, lemon bars, the coconut cream pie cut into triangles, the squares of bread pudding, the layered honey cake, an assortment of cookies, and the tray of raspberry galettes, your mother was not at all hungry. She wished that she would be overcome by one of the cravings for which pregnant women are famous, but she was not. When it was her turn to order she asked for a decaf coffee instead of the regular coffee that she wanted. Coffee was one of those pleasures that pregnant women claim to stop craving, but unfortunately your mother had not.

She carried the paper cup outside and sipped from it as she walked toward the station, the mid-December breeze carrying with it the cold smell of snow. She passed the row of boutiques, and without thinking twice, she stepped into the maternity shop, took the green dress from the rack, and carried it to the counter.

"It's for New Year's," your mother said, unzipping her wallet and avoiding the salesgirl's eyes. "I'll need more room by then."

The salesgirl remained silent as she rung up the dress and slipped a plastic bag over the hanger. She tied a knot at the bottom of the bag, then handed the dress to your mother.

Your mother rode the subway home, sitting by the dark window, lights flashing in the underground tunnel. It was hard for her to believe that you were there too, feeling on a microscopic level the same vibrations that she felt, the same sudden starts and stops of the train. It was only natural, of course, for her to have felt this way. You were her first child, and the reality of life within her was too abstract for her to fully comprehend.

That life can be created at all seems impossible. Of the 2.5 million sperm cells present in each release, only a fraction of a percent reach the ovum. Hundreds of thousands die on their way to the Fallopian tubes, and only half the survivors follow the tube where the ovum is secretly waiting. By the time the sperm reach the ovum, only an average of three hundred remain. Sperm cells can live inside the Fallopian tubes for three to five days, but the ovum has only twelve to twenty-four hours before it too is destroyed. If the ovum is present when the sperm enter the tube, or if it appears when the sperm are still alive, one sperm will burrow its way inside, causing the ovum's shell to harden and to shut the others out.

The chances of conception are 20 to 25 percent each cycle. But the probability of your conception—of the meeting of the particular sperm, one of your father's 2.5 million, with the particular ovum, one of your mother's three hundred thousand eggs—is inconceivable. In your mother's whole life, there were only twelve to twenty-four hours during which your existence could be made possible, and the possibility itself depended on so many variables. But somehow, these variables had lined up.

When she got home, your mother hung the dress in her closet, looking at it once more before turning off the light.

"How was the lecture?" your father asked, rummaging through the refrigerator for something to make for dinner.

"It was cancelled," your mother said. "But while I was in the neighborhood I bought a dress—for New Year's."

Your father set a block of cheese and a carton of eggs on the counter. "I suppose you'll be wanting to go to the party, then," he said, opening the low cupboard and reaching for an onion.

"We have to go," your mother said. "Nikolai's your most devoted client. And it's at that old, fancy supper club." She moved close to him, wrapping her arms around his waist from behind and pressing her cheek between his shoulder blades. "It'll be like going to a ball."

That night, when your father put his hand on your mother's breast in the dark, she didn't flinch. For the first time in weeks, her breasts were not too tender to touch, and without reserve your mother and father made love. Afterwards, your mother slept deeply, waking up inside another dream. She was strolling alongside your father in the park, late at night. The granite clock tower peeked out from behind the trees—its glowing face rimmed in gold, then blue. Your father was wearing a tuxedo, your mother her new green dress. As they walked, your mother holding onto your father's forearm, your mother noticed her flat stomach slowly beginning to expand, like a balloon filling with air. She held her hands on her growing stomach until she could no longer reach her arms around it. Then she began to feel very light, so light that, despite her expanding size, she floated off the ground. Your father gripped her hand, then her thigh, her knee, her ankle, and finally her foot, as she was lifted into the air. He was shouting something to her, but she couldn't hear him. She kept rising higher and higher into the sky, which turned suddenly warm and the color of blood. Then she saw you. Floating in your little amniotic bubble, you looked exactly as you had looked on the screen. A tiny white figure, moving all around. Your mother reached for you, but just before she touched you, you disappeared.

2

On New Year's Eve your father, dressed in his tux, was reading the paper on the living room sofa when your mother entered in a cap-sleeved black dress that stopped just below her knees. Your father looked up at her. "You're not wearing the green one?" he asked.

"I might as well wear my regular clothes while they still fit," your mother said. (She had never mentioned to your father what the woman had said at the boutique.) Twisting a tube of red lipstick, she looked into the mirror that hung above the mantel and applied the color to her lips. Then she walked to the closet, stepped into her heels, and slid her arms into her long, wool coat. "Are you ready?" she asked when she saw your father still sitting on the sofa.

"I suppose I have to be," your father said. He was not one for large parties.

Downstairs, on the street in front of their building, they flagged a taxi and got inside. It was snowing. The flakes shimmered beneath the streetlamps as they rode east toward the Slavic neighborhood.

The cab pulled up in front of the three-story brick building, its façade in need of mortar repair. Your father paid the driver, then followed your mother through the main entrance and into the crowded lobby. They stopped at the coat check before heading up the maroon-carpeted stairs that led to the ballroom.

A seven-piece jazz band was playing on the wooden stage, and an enormous chandelier sparkled above the dance floor. Two dozen large, round tables were draped in white cloths and set with plates, wine glasses, and silverware. In the center of each table sat a crystal vase arranged with blue hyacinths and white Casablanca lilies. Waiters everywhere were walking around, extending trays of bubbling champagne flutes toward the clusters of people drinking, laughing, and eating finger foods from small plates.

Your mother took a glass of champagne from a passing tray and handed it to your father. "I almost grabbed two," she said.

"Cheers," your father said, raising his glass. "May next year be as good to us as this year." He took a sip, and half the champagne was gone.

"Well?" your father said. "Shall we take a seat somewhere?"

"I'll just find the restroom first," your mother said. She left the ballroom through an open set of doors and followed the signs for the restroom.

It was an elegant room with royal blue wallpaper, gold filigree mirrors, brass faucets, and a marble floor. Your mother looked into one of the mirrors, checking her teeth for lipstick and smoothing her hair. Then she turned, glancing at her slim profile before stepping into one of the stalls.

She didn't have to go, but she sat down anyway, waiting there like a small child forced to try by her mother. After she went, just a trickle, she stood up and flushed, noticing a red mark on one of the tissues swirling around the bowl. It looked like a smear of lipstick, though she didn't remember blotting her lips. She sat back down on the seat and touched another bundle of tissue between her legs. On these sheets too she saw a spot, more rust-colored than red.

Your mother touched tissue after tissue between her legs, trying to get one that remained white, but the hint of blood kept appearing. She flushed the toilet and quickly washed her hands. Then she hurried to the ballroom for your father.

Searching the crowd, she found him off to the side, listening to the band and sipping from a fresh glass of champagne.

"We have to go," she said, taking his arm.

He looked at his watch. "Before dinner?"

"We have to go to the hospital," your mother said. "Now."

Outside, your father hailed the first taxi that passed. "The hospital," he said to the driver when he and your mother got into the back seat. "The emergency room entrance."

The driver took his place in the right lane, and one by one, all the lights turned green.

When they walked through the automatic sliding doors, your mother and father were met by a man in scrubs who led them to a woman sitting before a computer. Your mother sat down, and the woman began asking her a series of questions, beginning with her name. Your mother told her her name. Her reason for coming in? She was nine weeks pregnant, and she was having some bleeding. Any other symptoms? No. She felt perfectly fine.

A nurse appeared and took your mother's blood pressure and her temperature. She asked your mother to step on the scale, and she wrote down her weight. Then she left and came back with a wristband, which she fastened around your mother's left wrist before leading your mother and father down the stark white hallway to a stark white room. She handed your mother a gown that tied in the back and asked her to put it on. The doctor would be in shortly.

Your mother changed into the gown and sat down on the cot. Then your mother and father looked at the clock. It was 8:49 P.M. They looked at the cardboard box of blue masks hanging above the sink and at the hand sanitizer dispenser to its right. They looked at the closed cupboards made from cheap pine. They looked at the wires and plugs behind the cot, at the light switches and dimmers, at the turned-off television hanging from the ceiling in the left-hand corner of the room. It was still 8:49 P.M.

"Everything's going to be fine," your father said. "I'm sure of it."

"Well, I'm not," your mother said. "I won't be sure until I see her again on the screen. Just like I saw her last time. Only now she'll be bigger."

At 9:17, the doctor entered—a kind-looking man, not yet forty. "I'm Dr. Crowley," he said, reaching his hand to your mother, then across the cot to your father. He sat down on the wheeled stool. "I understand that you're experiencing some bleeding." He took some time to glance over the papers in his folder. "When did it start?"

"Tonight. I just noticed it."

Dr. Crowley looked at your mother. "A bit of spotting can be okay. The ultrasound will give us the most information." He looked again at his papers. "Before that we'll need to verify your blood type, get a urine sample, and check to see if your cervix is open or closed."

"What does it mean if it's open?" your mother asked.

"Miscarriage." Dr. Crowley stood up. "But we'll go there if we need to."

Soon after Dr. Crowley left, a man from the lab came to take blood. Then a nurse came in with a cup. Before long Dr. Crowley returned to check your mother's cervix. It was closed—a promising sign. Her blood tests came back. Her hemoglobin looked good. Her urine was fine, too.

"What could be causing the bleeding?" your mother asked Dr. Crowley, his hand on the doorknob.

"A number of things. The ultrasound will narrow the possibilities. We'll talk more when you return."

Ten minutes after Dr. Crowley had left, a nurse with a slight limp entered the room. She wheeled your mother's cot out the door and down the hallway, your father walking beside them, carrying your mother's purse. They went through a series of automatic doors, which lead to the main part of the hospital, and they entered the ultrasound unit. After parking your mother's cot alongside the wall, facing a closed door, the nurse waited quietly beside her.

A moment later the technician opened the door and wheeled another woman out. Resting her hands on her round stomach, the woman was smiling, and her cheeks were pink—glowing, your mother thought, because glowing is a trait that pregnant women possess. Then the nurse pushed the woman away, and the technician wheeled your mother, your father following close behind into the bluish, dimly lit room.

The technician sat down on the stool. She typed something into the computer and turned the screen away from your mother and toward herself. Then she stood up and squirted your mother's stomach with the goo from the bottle. This time it was warm. She touched the probe to your mother's stomach and began moving it around while watching the screen. She kept moving the probe and looking at the screen. Then she wiped your mother's stomach dry and slid a firm pillow beneath her lower back. "A bit of pressure," she said to warn your mother before inserting the other probe. Then the technician sat down on her stool, moving the probe inside your mother with one hand, while typing commands into the computer with the other. She kept her eyes on the screen.

The technician was young. No older than thirty. She had dark hair, cropped at her chin. Her skin was very pale, and she reminded your mother of Snow White. Your mother watched her face, which was serious and focused. Then your mother looked at the ceiling. Minutes passed. When she looked back at the technician, your mother was about to ask her if she'd found you, how you looked, how you seemed to be doing, but she didn't. She looked again at the ceiling instead.

At some point, it's hard to say when, your mother noticed that your father, who had been standing by her cot, watching the screen, was now sitting down on the chair in the corner of the room. The technician was taking photographs, many of them, a blip-blip sound every time she pressed a certain key.

"I'm going to take this out now," she said softly, removing the probe.

Your mother nodded, thinking that, for some perfectly acceptable reason, the technician was going to show her the photographs of you instead of showing you to her on the screen.

The technician looked into your mother's eyes. "I'm not seeing a heartbeat," she said.

Your mother stared at her, thinking that your heartbeat was merely hiding, because, for example, the chances of seeing a heartbeat every time one looked for it were not that high. Or because, at any particular moment, a heartbeat might not want to be seen. But it didn't make sense to your mother that, even though the technician's eyes were small, she couldn't find in them the confirmation she was looking for. She saw instead that the technician's eyes were shiny—glossy-looking. It wasn't until your mother heard your father crying quietly beside her that she realized the technician was crying too, though her tears weren't falling.

"I'm sorry," the technician said. She touched your mother's arm, then stood up, closing the door behind her and leaving your parents alone in the room.

You were still there, of course. Only your heartbeat wasn't. And your mother was beginning to put it all together.

There was a brief knock at the door, and a different nurse entered, this time a man. Reaching for the rail at the foot of the cot, he pulled your mother through the door and into the brightly lit hallway. Then he stepped behind your mother's head and pushed the cot forward, your father walking beside your mother and you floating somewhere inside her uterus.

The nurse was quiet as he wheeled your mother down the long hallway, through three sets of automatic doors and back into the stark white room. When he left, your father sat down. And after a while—neither your father nor mother had any concept of time by this point—Dr. Crowley returned and sat down on the stool beside your mother.

He began to explain that your mother would experience something similar to a heavy menstrual period. It would last for a few days. She might feel lightheaded, and if so, she should lie down. She would have some cramping, similar to the cramps she would feel were she having her period, though for some women they can be more severe. She should know that it wasn't anything that she had done or not done. There wasn't anything more that she could have done, or anything that she could have done instead. You had stopped growing at seven weeks and four days, and this was most likely due to a chromosomal abnormality, or to some problem that had occurred when, as a zygote, you underwent the process of division. With each pregnancy there's a 25 percent chance of miscarriage. What was happening to her was not uncommon.

Your mother looked at Dr. Crowley while he spoke. There were three faint lines on his forehead that she hadn't noticed before. And his curly hair seemed almost damp, as if it were very warm in the room, though your mother didn't notice any temperature at all.

Dr. Crowley stood up from the stool. He made some sweet attempt at a joke by referencing your mother's blood type—B positive. Then he looked at your parents once more before leaving the room.

"Seven weeks and four days," your mother said. She was looking at the ceiling. It was very smooth, and completely still. It looked so empty. Like a black hole, only it was white. "That's the day I saw her on the screen."

Your father was quiet. He had seen you on the screen for the first time just now. He had been waiting for your heart to flash as your mother had described for him again and again over the past two weeks. Like a turn signal that blinks really fast. Or a lightbulb that's constantly flickering. If it were a sound instead of a light, it would be a constant ticking—like a stopwatch pressed right to your ear.

"We should get home," he said to your mother, and at some point she sat up and began to dress.

1

In the morning, when your mother got out of bed, your father was sitting in the living room with a cup of coffee. He wasn't reading the paper, looking out the window, or listening to the radio. He was just sitting there, his coffee half full and cold. Your mother sat down beside him.

"I was thinking we should go to a movie," your father said. "A matinee will eat up some time."

At the theatre, your father paid for the tickets at the window outside. Then, taking off his hat, he held the glass door open for your mother. The previews were playing when he led her by the hand down the dark aisle toward an empty row on the right. Your mother slid in first, and your father took the aisle seat beside her.

The Latvian title of the movie appeared in white type—Futura heavy italic—on the dark screen, the English subtitle underneath. A moving truck pulled up to the curb as the names of actors were projected—one at a time in Futura light—the final name fading when your mother felt her first pain. She closed her eyes and grasped the armrests. The aching in her lower abdomen too sharp to allow her to breathe, she held her breath until the pressure began to decrease. Then she breathed and relaxed her hands. The screen now showed an empty living room—daylight pouring through the windows and shining on a hardwood floor, the bare white walls, the stack of boxes in the corner. Then another cramp began, this one more intense. Your mother grabbed your father's hand and squeezed it as hard as she could. She felt as if her insides were splitting open, and she clenched your father's hands so hard that she couldn't feel her fingers, slowly letting go sixty seconds later when the tension subsided.

When the third spasm erupted, your mother understood that she was having contractions. Her uterus was tightening then relaxing, tightening then relaxing, working to push you out, and there was nothing she could do to stop it. For the length of the movie, your mother squeezed your father's hand and breathed shallow breaths as you descended toward the birth canal, seven months too soon.

When the contractions had stopped and your mother felt that she could stand up, she held your father's arm and they headed up the slope of the aisle. The movie was over by this point, and the credits had run. As she walked, your mother felt something slipping, and only when she stepped into the restroom at the bookshop next door did she see that it was you. Lying in the hammock of her underwear and hidden inside the amniotic sac, covered in blood, you weren't quite an inch long, but your mother saw the line that was undoubtedly your spine.

Then, although she was imagining it, she saw you stretch, as if you had merely been asleep—the chimes of the clock tower outside just now waking you up. If this were a fairy tale, your mother would bathe you in a teacup, then set you in your walnut-shell cradle, covering you with a rose petal. And even though the fairy tale too separates you from your mother—carrying you on a swallow's back to a faraway land where you marry a prince as tiny as yourself—your mother asked that the story end here, at the part where you live happily ever after.